Lizard Flanagan,
Supermodel??

Also by Carol Gorman

THE MIRACULOUS MAKEOVER OF LIZARD FLANAGAN

CAROL GORMAN

Lizard Flanagan, Supermodel??

Best wishes to all the readers at Truman Elementary

Carol Gorman

2-7-03

■ HARPERCOLLINSPUBLISHERS

Library of Congress Cataloging-in-Publication Data
Gorman, Carol.
    Lizard Flanagan, supermodel?? / Carol Gorman.
        p.   cm.
    Summary: Anxious to earn money for an out-of-town baseball trip,
twelve-year-old sports-loving Lizard allows herself to be entered in a
contest to be a model in a fashion show, with unexpected results.
    ISBN 0-06-024868-8
    [1. Models (persons)—Fiction.]   I. Title.
PZ7.G6693Li   1998   97-49317
[Fic]—dc21   CIP
                                                                  AC

Typography by Becky James
1   2   3   4   5   6   7   8   9   10
❖
First Edition

To good friends:
Nancy Jennings,
Jacqueline Briggs Martin,
and Sharron McElmeel

Lizard Flanagan,

Supermodel??

CHAPTER ONE

"**NOW DO YOU BELIEVE ME,** Lizard?" said my best friend, Mary Ann Powers. "I told you I saw it. Isn't it fantastic?"

I unsnapped the chin strap of my bike helmet and stared at the poster. I wondered if I was dreaming. It seemed too good to be true. But there it was, hanging in the window of McCloud's Sporting Goods, printed in big red letters on a piece of white posterboard:

ATTENTION YOUNG BASEBALL FANS:
Join us on a trip to Wrigley Field to see the Chicago Cubs play!

WHEN: September 28

COST: $25 (includes grandstand tickets and bus trip)

FOR MORE INFORMATION, contact Shirley at City Park Recreation Department. Phone: 555-5630.

Mary Ann had told me last night on the phone that the poster was in the window, but I had to see it for myself. We'd started out early for school, and we took a one-mile detour to stop at McCloud's at the edge of Spring Pines Mall.

I leaned on my bike and reread the poster. "I can't believe it. This is great, really great."

Sports—especially baseball—are my life. I live for them. Mary Ann is a sports nut, too. We both played on the metro touch football and baseball leagues in elementary school, and we're going out for the Truman Middle School baseball team in the spring.

Mary Ann and I are the Cubs' biggest fans. But even though we live in Iowa, just five measly hours from Chicago, we've never seen a game in person at Wrigley Field. My brother, Sam, and I have been begging our mom and dad for three years to go, and they always say "Sure, sometime we'll do that." But it never happens.

Now I had my chance!

"We'll all go," Mary Ann said. "You, me, Sam, Zach, Ed, and Stinky." Zach is a fantastic athlete—last year he was voted MVP for

2

the Raiders, our metro flag football team, and he shared the MVP award with me on our baseball team, the Hawks. He's my best friend in the boy category. In fact, we're going out. Ed and Stinky are great friends of ours, too, and they play in the elementary metro leagues with the rest of us.

Mary Ann's smile got bigger. "Maybe Al will go too," she said, her face turning pink. Mary Ann's going out with Al Pickering, which I think is pretty funny. I mean, he's a great guy, but he was our archenemy when he QB'ed for the Cougars last year. Middle school has a way of mixing up old loyalties.

"You have a piece of paper?" I asked her.

She pulled off her backpack and rummaged through it before handing me a piece of paper torn from a spiral notebook.

"How about a pencil?"

This probably sounds crazy and superstitious, but I didn't want to move. I was afraid that if I budged even an inch, or looked away from the poster for too long, the spell would be broken and I'd wake up and realize it was only a dream.

I heard her pawing through her bag, and after half a minute more, she handed me a pencil whose point had been worn almost to the wood.

I copied the number and Shirley's name and let out a breath. I'd gotten it down on paper, and I hadn't awakened.

"I'll call the lady at the rec commission right after school," I said, folding the paper and shoving it into the pocket of my jeans. "This is so great! Come on. Let's go tell everybody."

"Yeah!"

I snapped the chin strap to my helmet, and we started off down the road. "How fast do you think I can go?" I called back to Mary Ann. "I bet I can do twenty-five miles an hour on this stretch."

"No way."

I grinned. "Just watch me, Powers, and don't open your mouth, or you'll eat my dust."

"Fat chance."

I pumped hard, standing on the pedals, keeping one eye on my new computerized speedometer. It's a beaut. It tells me my current speed and keeps track of any new records I set. It even has a clock and an odometer. After a whole lot of talking and a fair amount of pleading, I'd convinced Mom and Dad to advance me the twenty-five dollars from my allowance to get it. Of course, that also meant that I had to promise to do some crummy chores like cleaning out the garage and the basement to help earn the money to pay them back. So far, I'd only cleaned a corner of the basement, but I was planning on doing the rest fairly soon.

I pumped the pedals and changed from ninth to tenth gear, watching the numbers on the speedometer climb higher and higher. Twelve miles an hour, 13, 14. I glanced back at Mary Ann. She was about thirty yards behind, but I kept pushing. The stretch ended about a half mile ahead.

I was up to eighteen miles an hour now, and the grass along the curb was a green blur as I raced over the road. Nineteen, twenty, twenty-one miles an hour. This was the fastest I'd ever gone. I'd told Mary Ann I could go twenty-five miles an hour.

Mary Ann saw the truck before I did.

"Lizard!" she screamed behind me. *"Watch out!"*

I looked up and saw a truck pull onto the street ahead, not fifteen yards away.

I squeezed my brakes for all they were

worth, jerked the handlebars to the right, and spun around, my back tire sliding out from under me.

The driver of the truck saw me and jammed on his brakes just in time.

I heard the breath whoosh out of me as I hit the pavement, scraping my chin as I turned my head. I ended up on my side, just inches from the truck's back wheels.

The driver jumped out and bounded over to me.

"You okay?" His eyes were wild with fear.

I wasn't sure if I was okay or not. I moved my arms, then my legs. "Uh, yeah," I said. Actually, I was hurting all over and blinking back tears. I hadn't bawled in front of anyone since I was ten, though, and I wasn't going to let myself cry now.

"Lizard! Oh my gosh, I thought you were dead for sure!" Mary Ann stopped her bike in front of me. She was breathing hard. "Are you okay?"

"Sure."

I pulled myself to my feet, aching all over, and the guy's face suddenly changed from scared to angry. "What were you doing, trying to get yourself killed?"

I was about to say, No, that's generally not a goal I set for myself, but Mary Ann jumped right in.

"You know," she said to the man, "you pulled into traffic without making sure the street was clear, and my friend here is legally allowed to travel the speed limit, which is twenty-five miles an hour on this stretch. How fast were you going, Lizard?"

"Twenty-one."

The man waved angrily, marched back to the driver's seat and slammed the door behind him. Then he moved off down the road.

Mary Ann turned back to me and glared. "What were you doing, trying to get yourself killed?" she hollered. "Are you *crazy*?"

I was shaking all over, and my knees felt rubbery. It was a stupid thing to do, I knew that now, and I didn't plan on trying it again.

"I know, it was dumb," I said. "But I'm okay."

"Good thing you were wearing your helmet," Mary Ann said.

"I didn't hit my head."

"You could have split it right open, just like a watermelon."

I didn't want to think about that. "Come on, let's go."

My bike was scraped, but it worked. I climbed back on and started off down the road. I'd probably need to get the brakes adjusted, but for now I could get to school with no problem.

"Your chin's bleeding," Mary Ann said, coming up from behind. "Your arm is too. And your jeans are torn."

"Yeah, I know. I'll clean up at school."

Mary Ann didn't say any more. Maybe she knew I was more shaken up than I let on. She has a special radar for that kind of stuff.

We got to school and parked our bikes.

"Hey, Lizard! Mary Ann! Over here!" It was Ginger Flush, my locker partner.

Everybody at Truman Middle School shares a locker with one other person of the same sex. It's according to the alphabet, so my locker partner is Ginger because her last name begins with *Fl*, just like mine. She's also—and I don't admit this to very many people—going out with my brother, Sam. What he sees in her is one of the biggest mysteries of my life.

Ginger hurried over. Standing nearby was

Lisa St. George, the most sickeningly gorgeous girl in the sixth grade. Ginger is Lisa's sidekick. You know, like Robin is to Batman. Whenever you see Lisa coming into a room, you know that Ginger's not far behind. It's funny, though; even though Ginger's the sidekick, she talks a lot more than Lisa.

Ginger stopped in front of me. "We're all making guesses on who—" She stopped and stared at my chin. "Hey, Lizard, do you know you're bleeding all over the place?" She pointed to a spot of blood on my shoulder. "Gross!"

I shrugged. "My bike fell out from under me."

She frowned. "Bruises and scars for sure."

Lisa stepped forward, looking impatient. "We're all making guesses about who will make the first cut to model in the Spring Pines fashion show. We're making lists of everyone's guesses, then tomorrow after school when the names are posted, we'll find out who was right."

"What are you talking about?" I asked.

Ginger's eyes got big. "You mean you haven't heard about the fashion show?

Everybody at school has been talking about it for weeks!"

I shrugged.

"It's the biggest event of the year!" Ginger said. "Almost every girl in school sent in a head shot—that's a close-up picture of your face—and a bio telling about her interests and stuff. My sister said lots of girls in the high school did too. First, about twenty-five girls will get picked to go on to the interviews. After that, fourteen girls—two from every grade, sixth through twelfth—will be chosen to model in the fashion show. They'll each get fifty dollars, and the best model in the show will be picked as Spring Pines Mall's Supermodel. She'll get a hundred dollars!"

"So we're guessing who'll be on the first list?" Mary Ann asked. Ginger's head waggled up and down.

"I'll make a guess," Mary Ann told Ginger.

"I'm going inside to clean up," I said to Mary Ann. "If I see the guys, I'll tell them about the Cubs game."

I started off toward the building and heard Mary Ann say, "I bet you'll be chosen, Lisa."

"That's eighty-three guesses for me," Lisa

said. I could hear the smugness in her voice from ten yards away.

I walked stiffly through the crowd of kids waiting to get into the school, trying not to limp. My right leg felt as if someone had slammed it with a baseball bat. My jeans were torn clear through at the knee, but the skin wasn't even scraped. I pulled open the door to the school building.

"Hey, Lizard!" I recognized Zach Walters's voice.

"Hi, Zach." I turned and grinned at him, then let the door swing closed again. "Boy, do I have great news for you."

"For me?" He walked over, followed by my twin brother, Sam, Ed Mechtensteimer, and Stinky Porter.

"Great news for all of us. We're going to Chicago to see a Cubs game!"

"We are?"

"What are you talking about?" Sam asked.

"Hey, Lizard," Zach said, looking at my chin. "What happened? You're bleeding."

"I fell off my bike," I said. "Some guy driving a truck practically killed me. And I was about to break my all-time speed record, too. If the guy hadn't cut me off, I could've made it up to twenty-five miles an hour for sure!"

Sam's face didn't change. "The trucker may not have killed you, but Mom will when she hears about it."

I ignored my brother. "Hey, listen, there's going to be a trip to Wrigley Field in a couple of weeks to see the Cubbies play!"

"You're kidding!" Zach said.

"The Cubs? The Chicago Cubs?" Ed said. "You're sure?"

"No way," Stinky said. "You're making that up."

"I saw the poster with my very own eyes. It's hanging in McCloud's window. The trip costs twenty-five dollars, and that's for box seats and the bus ride. I suppose we have to bring extra money for Cokes and hot dogs and stuff to eat along the way. You have to call someone named Shirley at the City Park Recreation Department to sign up. Here, I have the number."

I dug in my pocket and pulled out the piece of paper.

"It'd be better if we could see the Yankees play," Ed said.

"Who'd want to see the Yankees?" I said.

Zach took the paper and started to copy down the number on the front cover of his social studies notebook.

"Hey, don't you guys start arguing about the Yankees and the Cubs again," Stinky said.

"I just wish," Ed said, "that if I got to see a major-league game, it'd be in New York."

"Well, you can stay home, Mechtensteimer," I said. "If you can't appreciate the talent on the Cubs' team—"

"Aren't you forgetting just one thing, Lizard?" Sam asked.

"What?"

"The fifty dollars it will cost for the two of us. Where are we going to get that much money?"

"Where do you think? From Mom and Dad."

Sam looked at me as if I'd said something really dumb. "You think they'll hand over fifty bucks so we can see a baseball game? No way!"

"They won't just *give* it to us," I said patiently. "They'll advance us the money from our allowance."

"Mom'll never go for that. It's too much money."

"Just you wait," I said. "I know Mom and Dad better than you do—"

"*What?*"

"They'll let us go out of guilt," I told him. "They know how long we've been wanting to go to a Cubs game, see? It's an easy way to make them feel better for not taking us all these years."

"Oh." Sam looked as if he finally understood. "Well, maybe."

Zach grinned. "We'll have such a great time, sitting at Wrigley Field, eating hot dogs and popcorn, and watching Mark Grace play first base."

"Yeah," I said. "Wouldn't it be great if a fly ball came right at us? I'm going to take my mitt for sure!"

The bell rang, and we headed inside with all the other kids. I said good-bye to the guys and headed to the rest room. When I looked in the mirror over the sink, I was surprised at how banged up I looked. There were two scrapes on my chin, both starting to scab over, and dried blood was smeared on my shirt. My right arm was scraped, too, from my wrist up to my elbow.

I washed my face with a paper towel, and

the scratches on my chin started bleeding again.

I stopped in at the nurse's office on my way to language arts class, and she cleaned my chin again and put on a bandage.

"That's a nasty scrape on your arm, too," she said. "You'll have to be more careful riding your bike."

"Yeah." *At least, I'd have to ride fast on quieter streets*, I thought to myself.

I went through my morning classes doing two things: (1) explaining to everybody how I got scraped and bloody, and (2) daydreaming about watching the Chicago Cubs play in person at Wrigley Field. I'd dreamed about that a lot in my life, and now I was actually going to do it!

The sixth grade at Truman is divided into two groups, orange and black, the colors for the Truman Tigers. Everybody in the same group goes through their classes together. I'm in the orange group with Ed and Stinky. Mary Ann, Zach, and Sam are in the black group.

At lunch, though, everything is scrambled, and I get to see some of my friends in the black group. At five minutes after twelve

I hurried to the cafeteria, as usual, to eat lunch with Zach, Ed, and Stinky. They were standing together in the hall, just outside the cafeteria door. Mike Herman and Andy Walinsky were there too.

"Hey, guys," I greeted them. "I can't stop thinking about the game. I'm going to see if I can get Mark Grace to sign my glove."

"That would be so great," Zach said, grinning.

"What're you guys talking about?" Mike asked. We told him about the trip to Chicago.

"The Cubs are horrible," Mike said. "Especially since Ryne Sandberg resigned."

"Oh, yeah?" I shot back. "Well, the Cubbies still have Mark Grace, the world's greatest first baseman. He's a Golden Glove winner and has more RBIs—"

Zach joined in. "And don't forget Sammy Sosa, their right fielder. He's making big bucks 'cause he's so talented."

"Wow, and just think," I said, grinning. "We'll be seeing these guys *in person.*"

We got in line for lunch. "I'm going to buy a Chicago Cubs jersey," I said.

"You already have one," Stinky said.

"I already have *three*," I corrected him.

"But none of them came from Wrigley Field!"

Just then, Ginger, Lisa, and Tiffany Brady arrived. Ginger beamed as they approached. "Oh, look who's here! More people for our poll!" They stopped in line behind us, and Ginger held up her hands. "Okay, you guys. We're conducting a poll: Which of the girls from our sixth grade class do you think will make the first cut to model in the Spring Pines Mall fashion show? Ed, you first."

Ed grinned and shrugged. "I didn't know about it. The Spring Pines—what is it?"

"The fashion show!" Ginger said. "Haven't you heard about it?"

"Nope." He grinned like an idiot, looking back and forth between Lisa and Ginger.

"Well, think of the girls in our class," Ginger said. "Two of them will get chosen to model in the fashion show. So name at least one girl who you think will get picked."

"I dunno." Ed continued to grin and look dumb. I wanted to smack him.

Ginger slowed down so that Ed would be able to comprehend what she was saying. "Well, who do you think is the most beautiful girl in the sixth grade?" She and Lisa and Tiffany leaned in to hear his answer.

I didn't think it was possible, but Ed's grin got even bigger. "Ṣara Pulliam."

"Sara Pulliam," Ginger said to Lisa, who held the notebook.

Lisa's jaw got tight, and she wrote down Sara's name. "Of course he'd say Sara," she huffed. "He's going out with her. Some people just can't be objective."

I paid the cashier. "Come on, you guys," I said. "You're holding up the line." I picked up a dish of red Jell-O with apples in it and started through the cafeteria line.

"Hey, Lizard." Ginger paid the cashier and tiptoed around the guys to me. She leaned in and whispered, "Do you think Sam would vote for me?" She giggled.

"I don't know," I said. "Why don't you ask him?"

She laughed. "Oh, I'd die before I'd ask him!" She whirled around and leaned over to talk to Tiffany, who was standing behind the guys. "*You* ask Sam, Tiff. We'll see him in the hall after sixth period."

We inched along the lunch line. I picked up a small dish of green beans and put them on my tray. One of the cooks, dressed in a white uniform and a hairnet, handed me a plate with a sloppy joe on it.

"Who do you think will be chosen to model, Zach?" Ginger asked. "Give me at least one name."

I held my breath and stared at my Jell-O, waiting for his answer. Zach and Lisa had gone out for a couple of weeks at the very beginning of school, but he'd been going out with me since they broke up. I hoped Zach wouldn't vote for Lisa.

"I don't know," Zach said. "I can't guess."

"Leave your emotions out of it," Lisa counseled him. "Just think of the prettiest face you can imagine." She cocked her head, opened her eyes wide, and—I'm not kidding—fluttered her lashes at him.

Zach looked away from her, and his ears turned bright red. "I vote for Lizard."

Stinky laughed. "Oh, man," he said, rolling his eyes.

Lisa snorted. *"What?"*

Zach looked her directly in the eye. "I said Lizard."

Ginger beamed. "Zach, that's so *nice* of you!"

I wished I could've vaporized into the air. "I didn't send in my picture, Zach," I murmured.

Lisa laughed. "With that bandage on her face, Lizard's a *really* dumb choice. Models don't go out on the runway looking like accident victims."

"Come on," Zach said to me, taking his plate from the cook and motioning with his head. "Let's go sit down."

I knew my face was bright red. It was so hot you could've fried an egg on it. Lisa was such a jerk! So what if I wasn't gorgeous like Lisa. I wasn't so bad looking. I'd recently learned how to put my hair in a French braid and how to put on some blush, and sometimes I think I look pretty good. Boys even turn to look at me occasionally.

Zach and I sat at our table, and Ed followed.

"Stinky's voting in the poll," Ed said. "He'll be right here."

"Those girls are so stupid," Zach said.

"Do you think one of the girls from our class will get to be a model?" Mike asked, looking at me.

"Who cares?"

Mike looked disappointed, so I added, "Ginger said they're picking fourteen girls— two from each grade."

Stinky arrived with his lunch and sat down.

"Who'd you vote for, Stink?" Ed asked him. Stinky shrugged. "Come on," Ed said. "You heard *my* vote."

"Aw, you were just voting for your girlfriend," Stinky said. "They wanted an objective answer."

"So who do you think will get to model?" Ed asked him.

"Lisa, of course," Stinky said. "She's *stacked*."

I dropped my fork. "You make me sick, Stinky. Models don't have to have big . . . chests. They're thin all over."

"Oh, yeah?" Stinky said. "Do you ever look at the *Sports Illustrated* swimsuit issue? Man-oh-man-oh-man!"

Ed, Mike, and Andy laughed, and even Zach grinned.

"Well, just because a girl looks good in a swimsuit, it doesn't mean she's interesting or fun to be with!"

"Know what I say to that, Lizard?" Stinky said with a devilish grin. "Who cares?"

"Well, I just happen to know," I said, "that the girls who applied to model in the fashion show sent in pictures of their *faces* and information about their lives. That's all."

Stinky grinned wickedly. "They didn't have to tell their bra size?"

"Some of the girls don't even wear bras," Ed informed him.

"How would you know *that,* Mechten-steimer?" I could hear myself yelling, but I didn't care.

Ed smiled smugly. "I can tell."

Stinky laughed. "So can I. Any guy can."

"You jerks must be looking pretty *hard,*" I said.

Stinky hooted. "We are!" His gaze went right to my chest.

I stood up, my cheeks blazing hot. "You creep!" I gave him a hard shove, and he nearly fell off the bench.

"Hey, where're you going?" Ed said.

"Away from you and Stinky. I've lost my appetite."

"Good going, guys," Zach said to them.

I pulled my book bag out from under the table, and stormed out of the cafeteria and down the hall, fuming. Someday, I swear, I'm going to strangle Stinky Porter.

I stopped near the doorway of a darkened classroom and leaned against the wall. I forced myself to think about the Wrigley Field trip. That made me feel better. Maybe Stinky would get a cold or the plague or something and not be able to go with us.

I couldn't wait to go home after school and get the trip money from Mom and Dad. Then I'd call Shirley and reserve my place on the bus.

Yes, I thought. *That would make me feel a whole lot better.*

CHAPTER TWO

THE BEST TIME TO ASK Mom and Dad for anything is after supper. They come home tired from work, and they don't feel like doing much but changing into their jeans and fixing supper. I've learned from experience that they're more likely to agree to stuff if I wait till after supper. They're in better moods then, more relaxed and more likely to say yes!

It was Mom's night to cook. I was determined to eat whatever healthy food she put in front of me, no matter how terrible it was. She's a health nut and likes to fix food that most people would throw in the garbage, dishes that have ingredients like bulgur wheat or brewer's yeast or wheat germ. I'm not even positive those things are meant to be eaten. I like a healthy snack once in a while for variety, but Mom goes way overboard.

Tonight she'd fixed Tomato Quiche with Egg Beaters on a whole wheat crust. I'd rather have had pizza, but compared with some of Mom's disasters—the worst was Spinach and Mustard Greens Soup—it wasn't too horrible. I managed to choke it down without resorting to my B.A.R.F. Plan. B.A.R.F. stands for Ban All Revolting Foods. It means that I do whatever's necessary to avoid eating Mom's cooking, even if I have to feed the stuff to my dog, Bob, under the table.

I'd gotten Sam to promise to let me handle the Chicago trip. He would've just blurted out, "Can we have fifty bucks to go to a Cubs game?" He doesn't understand that you have to use finesse to get what you want.

I first learned about finesse the time I watched Zach talk his mother into letting him go camping with my family. He'd asked her a week before, and she'd said no. She wanted him to help her paint the living room.

Zach told her about a boy at the high school who'd gotten caught breaking into Jim's Audio and Video.

"What a shame," Mrs. Walters said. She was shelling peas on the back porch. The

25

peas *ping*ed into the steel pan on her lap. "He's throwing his life away, and he doesn't even know it."

"I wonder what starts people down the road to crime?" Zach said. He popped a couple of raw peas into his mouth.

"Part of it," said his mother, "is that friends and families just don't spend as much time together doing wholesome activities the way they used to. Kids are left to roam the streets without adult supervision."

Zach nodded. "Yeah. I wish I could spend more time doing stuff with our family—and Lizard's. You know, like hiking and camping and doing stuff in nature."

"I know," his mom said. "We should make more time for the great outdoors, shouldn't we? We get so busy."

"It gets pretty boring sometimes, roaming the streets or hanging out with Stinky," Zach said. Mrs. Walters doesn't exactly love Stinky. She winced, and the corners of her mouth tightened a little. Zach looked at me. "Lizard, aren't you going on vacation pretty soon?"

"Yeah, we're camping at Backbone State Park."

"That sounds like fun," Mrs. Walters said.

"I sure wish you could come with us, Zach," I said pointedly. "Mom said to be sure to invite you."

"Thanks, but I'm going to help Mom paint. And I told Stinky I'd hang out with him in the evenings."

Mrs. Walters sat up straight and looked thoughtful. "Oh, I think you'd have a much better time on a camping trip with the Flanagans, Zach," she said. "We'll paint when you get back."

"But I promised Stinky."

"Zach, I want you to go with Lizard's family," she said firmly. "I'm sure your dad will agree."

Zach flashed me a quick smile. "Well, okay."

I was really impressed, and I asked him later where he'd learned his technique.

"My cousin Anthony," he said. "He's the master of finesse. It's pretty sneaky, so I only resort to it when it's really important."

It was sneaky, all right. But if a kid only used it in emergencies, it seemed okay to me.

So tonight I was going to try using some

finesse. An opportunity to see a Cubs game definitely qualified as an emergency situation.

First, I played up my accident—being sure to emphasize how careless the driver of the truck had been. I didn't mention that I'd been flying along at twenty-one miles per hour. Mom and Dad were very concerned about me, but I assured them that I was— probably—okay.

"Could you pass the quiche?" I asked Dad. "Ow, my arm is awfully sore."

"That's okay, hon," Dad said. "I'll serve you a piece."

"Not too much," I said. "My chin hurts a little when I chew."

"I'll take a look under that bandage later," Mom said.

Now, in case you're starting to feel sorry for my mom and dad, I wasn't acting too much. I really was sore all over, and it did hurt to reach out my arm. I just played it up a little.

Since Mom had cooked, Dad cleaned up. I opened my mouth to offer to help with the dishes but stopped myself just in time. *Don't go overboard*, I told myself. I'd have to act natural, or they'd get suspicious. I had to wait to be asked, then complain just a little.

"Come on, Lizard, Sam," Dad said, pushing back his chair from the table. "Let's get that mess cleaned up in the kitchen. I have bowling tonight."

Oh, shoot. I'd forgotten. Dad bowls in a league from his office twice a month, and tonight was the night.

It was going to be hard to get Mom and Dad together to finesse them both at the same time. It looked as if I'd have to start with Dad.

"You guys put the food away, and I'll start washing," Dad said as we walked into the kitchen.

We started to work, and then, I swear, he handed me an opening.

"So how's school going?" Dad asked.

"Okay," Sam said.

I was covering the quiche with plastic wrap. I looked up. "Oh—" I paused for a little drama. "Okay—I guess."

Dad glanced over at me. "Anything wrong?"

"Well, it's just that it's hard to meet people. Sometimes I feel kind of lonely."

"*What?*" Sam said, sounding surprised. I

threw him a dish towel and gave him a meaningful glance.

"I thought you knew half the boys at school from your ball teams," Dad said, up to his elbows now in suds.

"Well, I know *some* of them," I said. "It's hard to get to know the girls, though. They're all in cliques."

"Didn't you go to a slumber party a couple of weeks ago?" Dad asked.

"Those girls are kind of stupid," I said. "I wish I knew more girl jocks like Mary Ann and me." I paused again. "There's one thing coming up that sports lovers, guys and girls, will sign up for. That might be a chance to meet people."

"What's that?"

"A trip to Chicago to see the Cubs," I said. "At the end of September."

"Wow," Dad said, rinsing off a plate, "that sounds like a trip made for you."

"It sure does," I said, grinning at Sam. "And it only costs twenty-five dollars. Just think, a chance to make new friends and see a Cubs game for so little money!"

"Sounds great," Dad said.

"Yeah, it would be great if Sam and I could

both go," I said. "We can pick up a lot of pointers for the school baseball team."

"Terrific."

I held up my fists in victory to Sam. He gave me a silent high five behind Dad's back.

We were going to see the Cubs game!

Mom walked into the kitchen.

"What're you two grinning about?" she asked. She put some folded towels in the drawer.

"We're just happy," I said. "Sam and I are going to see a Cubs game at the end of the month. Dad said we could go."

"A Cubs game?" Mom said. "Who's taking you?"

I explained about the sign in the window at McCloud's.

"Twenty-five dollars?" Mom said. "Where are you going to get the money?"

I stopped and stared at her. "Uh, I thought you could advance us the money from our allowance."

"No way," Mom said. "We just advanced you twenty-four ninety-five for that computerized speedometer."

"But, Mom—" Panicked, I looked at Dad. "Dad said we could go!"

"You didn't tell me that you'd have to get the money in advance," Dad said. "Don't you have anything in your savings account?"

"Nope," Sam said. "That's why she needed the twenty-five-dollar advance for the speedometer."

"Oh, shut up, Sam!"

Sam looked at Mom. "I have nearly twenty dollars saved. Could I have an advance on the rest? It'd only be five bucks or so."

"We'll see."

"*What?*" I cried. "You'd let Sam go and not me?"

"Lizard," Mom said, "you need to learn a lesson in saving. When you spend all your money on baseball cards and sports equipment, you don't have anything saved for special occasions that come up, like this trip to Chicago."

"But I'm the biggest Cubs fan in the whole world!" I said. "Baseball is my life!" Then I tried a new tack. "I could take my speedometer back to the store and get a refund."

"Not this time," Mom said. "You'd still be twenty-five dollars in debt." She looked at Dad. "Agreed?"

"You bet."

"But there won't *be* a next time," I said. "I'll pay you back fast. I'll do extra work to earn it."

"I'm sorry, Lizard," Mom said. "But you haven't even started paying back the twenty-four ninety-five. I'm not going to let you dig yourself even deeper in debt."

"But, Mom—"

"Do you know how long it would take you to pay us back fifty dollars?" Dad stopped me. "You get six dollars a week in allowance. It would take you more than two months to earn that much. And during that time, you'd probably think of five other things you *had* to have."

"Lizard," Mom said. "I know you love the Cubs. Why don't we plan to see a game next summer? The whole family will go."

"But that's almost a year away!"

"In the meantime, you can watch them on TV." Mom headed out of the kitchen.

I followed. "But, Mom—"

She whirled around in the dining room and glared at me. "That's it, Lizard. The answer is no. Don't bring it up again."

"I—"

"*No.* You understand? End of discussion."

Mom walked out of the room. I was stunned. I felt as if I'd been hit with a sledge-hammer.

My dream of sitting in the stands at Wrigley Field, watching my heroes play base-ball, was gone like a wisp of smoke.

Everyone would be there without me. Even Sam, that rat. He'd come home and tell me every wonderful detail about the game and say, "You should've been there, it was so great."

And I'd think, *You bet I should've been there, you rat.*

I went upstairs, flopped on my bed and stared out the window.

If only I had the money!

That's when I decided it. This wasn't over yet! I wasn't going to be beaten this easily. There *had* to be a way to get to the Cubs game!

Twenty-five dollars was a lot of money, and I didn't know how I'd come up with it.

"But I'll get it," I promised myself out loud. "Somehow, I'll find a way to get that money. I *will* see the Cubs play."

CHAPTER THREE

THE SKY WAS AS BLACK as my mood the next day. I was still determined to find a way to get the money I needed, but my anger at Mom and Dad continued to run through my body.

We live too close to school to be eligible to ride the school bus, so whenever the weather was bad Mom drove Mary Ann, Sam, and me before she went to work. The windshield wipers slapped at the raindrops as Mary Ann slid into the backseat next to me.

"If it's still raining after school, Lizard, you and Sam can take the city bus home. Here." Mom dug into her bag with her right hand and came up with two dollar bills and four quarters. "Do you need some bus money, Mary Ann?"

"No, thanks," she said. "My dad gave me some this morning."

Mary Ann looked uncomfortable. I'd called her last night to tell her that Mom and Dad wouldn't let me go to the Cubs game. Her mom had just given her permission. Mary Ann knew I was still very angry; I had barely said a word since she'd gotten into the car.

She looked out the window.

"Lizard," Mom said, "good luck on your math test."

"Thanks." I said it curtly and refused to look at her.

"What else is on tap for today?" she asked.

I didn't answer.

"Lizard?"

"Don't bother trying to talk to her," Sam said. "She's pouting."

"Shut up, Sam," I said.

"It's nobody's fault but your own that you can't go to the Cubs game," he said. "If you didn't blow all your money—"

"I don't blow all my money!" I said. Of course, that was a lie, but I was itching for a fight.

"Oh, yeah?" Sam said. His eyes went into

little slits like they always do when he's mad and acting like a jerk. "So why is your savings account empty, and mine has nearly twenty dollars in it?"

"I need more stuff than you do. Besides, you're really cheap—you're always bumming quarters off Zach and Mary Ann and me for the candy machine at Whetstone's!"

"I don't bum quarters!" he yelled. "Do I, Mary Ann?"

"Don't speak to him, Mary Ann!" I told her.

"All right," Mom cut in, "that's enough."

"She's acting like a baby," Sam said.

"And you're acting like a jerk," I said.

"Stop it!" Mom said.

Mary Ann probably wished she'd walked in the rain. No one spoke the rest of the way. At school, I got out of the car, slammed the door, and sprinted into the building. Mary Ann followed close behind.

The kids were all crowded into the foyer. The floor was wet with tracked-in rain, and the air smelled of damp hair and—I sniffed again. *Yuck.* It was that mushy goulash the cooks make for lunch about four days a week.

Zach waved at us from the side of the foyer.

"Come on," I said to Mary Ann. We weaved our way through the crowd to Zach, who stood with Ed and Stinky. Their hair was soaking wet and matted to their heads, and beads of water dripped off their rain slickers.

"Hey, Lizard," Zach said, grinning. "You got the bandage off your chin. Those scrapes don't look too bad."

"I can't go to Chicago, Zach."

His face darkened. "You can't?"

"Mom and Dad won't advance me the money. Sam's probably going, though."

"Oh, shoot," he said. "It won't be as much fun without you. You still going, Mary Ann?"

"I don't know," she said. "I'm not sure I'll go without Lizard."

"Well, I'm going," Stinky said.

"Me, too," said Ed. He wasn't even a Cubs fan! *Life can be so unfair,* I thought.

I sagged against the wall.

Zach stared off into the distance. "Something like this happened once to my cousin Wally." He got that funny look in his eyes that comes just before one of his stories.

"Another cousin?" Stinky smirked. But he leaned in to listen. Everybody loves to hear Zach tell his stories.

"Yeah," Zach said. "What Wally wanted more than anything was to go to World-O-Rama and ride on the biggest, wildest roller coaster in the state. It's all inside a gigantic spook house, where ghosts and goblins come after you in the dark, and you spin in three-hundred-sixty-degree turns, and you get splashed with water and screamed at by demons."

"Cool," Ed murmured, his eyes wide.

"It *was* cool, and it was all Wally thought about," Zach said. "The idea kind of scared him, but he was obsessed. He wanted to be able to say he'd survived the Demons' Den. He even dreamed about it at night, and woke up in a cold sweat, shaking all over.

"Finally, he had his chance to go. His scoutmaster announced that they'd all be taking a trip to World-O-Rama. It only cost twenty-five dollars apiece."

"Just like the Cubs game," I said.

"Yeah," Zach said. "But his parents wouldn't give him the money, either."

"What did he do?" Mary Ann asked.

"He heard about this weird old woman who granted wishes. She lived in a shack next to the railroad tracks, and Wally went to see her.

"'I need twenty-five dollars to go to World-O-Rama,' Wally said. 'I want to ride through the Demons' Den.'

"'No problem,' she said, 'but you have to do one thing for me first. Bring me a lock of your principal's hair.'

"Wally was stunned. His principal was the meanest, rottenest woman in the whole state. How would he ever get a lock of her hair? 'Couldn't I slay a dragon instead?' he asked.

"'Bring me a lock of her hair,' the old woman said. 'Then you will have the money you need.'

"Wally lay awake at night trying to figure out how he could get a lock of his principal's hair. Should he slip a sleeping potion into her coffee and sneak up on her after she fell asleep in the teachers' lounge? No, that was too risky. Teachers were always coming into the lounge; he was sure to get caught. He even thought of running up to her, grabbing a fistful of hair, lopping off some of it and running away. He didn't know what the punishment was for stealing hair, but maybe a trip to World-O-Rama would make it worthwhile.

"But then he got the Idea, and he wondered why he hadn't thought of it before. He strolled up to the principal the next day and said, 'Excuse me, Ms. Hardnose, but my mom's looking for a new haircutter. Your hair looks pretty good. Who cuts it?'

"Wally heard a funny creaking sound as Ms. Hardnose's face twisted itself into a smile. It was the first smile her face had ever made. 'Why, Wally, what a nice compliment,' she said. 'I get my hair cut by Susie down at Chez Hair.'

"So that's how Wally got a lock of her hair. He just hung around Chez Hair until Ms. Hardnose's next appointment, then asked Susie if he could have some of the hair on the floor for a science project." Zach grinned. "He went to World-O-Rama and had the time of his life. He even got a T-shirt that said, I SURVIVED THE DEMONS' DEN."

"Aw, he should've just whacked off a lock of Hardnose's hair and run away," Stinky said. "That's what I would've done."

"Right, Stinky," Ed said, rolling his eyes.

"I'd like to see you do that to Wildwoman." Mary Ann and Zach laughed at the thought. Our principal, Mrs. Wildman (or Wildwoman, as the kids call her), is about six foot two, and Stinky's pretty short. "You'd need a stepladder to get to her head."

"I wish I knew a weird old woman down by the railroad tracks," I said. "I'd do anything to get the money."

Zach stared off thoughtfully. "Maybe something will come up, and it'll be easier than you think. Just like it was for Wally."

"Wouldn't that be great, Lizard?" Mary Ann said.

It sure would. But I didn't know what could possibly come up that would help me get the money.

The bell rang, and we trooped into the hall. I said good-bye to Mary Ann and the guys and headed for my locker.

Ginger Flush was pawing through her stuff when I got there. She turned around and beamed.

"Lizard, isn't it exciting? Today's the day!"

"What day?"

Her mouth dropped open. "Are you kidding? Today the first cut for the Spring

Pines fashion show will be posted!"

"Oh. Right." I shoved my math book inside the locker and took out my stuff for language arts.

She giggled. "I can't believe you forgot! I could hardly sleep last night. I kept wondering who, besides Lisa, will get chosen! Of course, I hope it'll be me, but the competition will be really tough!" She grabbed my arm. "Hey, we're all going over to the mall together after school to see the list of names. Want to come with us?"

"I'll probably have homework or something." I pulled my arm away.

"Oh, come on," Ginger said. "Everybody who's anybody will be there."

I stared at her. I wanted to say, "Like I'd care?" but I knew it would sound really rude, so I kept quiet.

"We need moral support," Ginger continued. "Lisa doesn't act nervous, but she's really a mess. Tiffany's been biting her nails more than usual, and I haven't been able to eat for two days! Just think how great it would be for Sam if I was picked. He'd be so happy for me!"

I wondered why it would be great for Sam

if Ginger was on the list. "Thanks anyway," I said.

"But, Lizard, don't you want to know who made the first cut? The girls on the list go on to the interview."

"No, thanks. I hope you win." She squealed at the thought.

I wasn't in the mood to listen to any more. Who cared about modeling and fashion shows? I couldn't think of anything more boring than that. I headed to my first class.

Ginger wasn't the only person with a one-track mind that day. In language arts, our teacher, Ms. Pearl Yeck, asked Christine Mulray to make up a sentence with at least one prepositional phrase. Chris thought a few seconds and said, "After school, I'm going to the mall to read the posting of the first cut for the fashion show."

"Excellent," Squirrely Pearly said. Squirrely Pearly is what we call Ms. Yeck behind her back, and the name fits her perfectly. We spend more time fooling around in her class than learning. "How many prepositional phrases were in that sentence, Marcy?"

Marcy Olson grinned. "I don't know, but

I'm going to the mall, too."

"Lisa St. George is sure to get picked," Chris said. "Ginger Flush took a survey, and she got ninety-five percent of the votes."

"That's because Lisa was hovering over everyone polled," Ed said, "giving them a death stare."

That cracked everyone up, including Squirrely.

"It'll be fun to find out who's on the list," Squirrely said. "Come and tell me tomorrow."

About fifteen girls vowed to be first in the building tomorrow to tell her.

"I'll come back after school this afternoon," Marcy said, "and tell you who's on the list."

I rolled my eyes. It amazed me how these people could get so excited about a stupid fashion show. Compared to a baseball or basketball or football game, a fashion show was a total yawn fest!

"You going to walk over to the mall to see the posting?" Mary Ann asked me after school. She'd met me at my locker.

"Are you kidding? That's all anyone talked about today, and I'm sick of it."

"What are you going to do instead?"

"Go home."

"And do what?"

"I don't know."

"Lizard, you know you'll just go home and feel sad about not being able to go to Chicago. Why don't you come with me to the mall?"

"Why do you want to go?" I asked her. "Who cares who's picked for that stupid fashion show?"

"It's the list of the people chosen to go on to the interview," Mary Ann corrected me.

"Whatever."

"I think it'll be interesting to see who's chosen. Come on, at least it'll take your mind off the trip for a while."

She had a point. Zach had a dentist's appointment after school, and with Mary Ann gone, there wouldn't be enough people to get up a ball game.

I sighed. "Okay. I guess there's nothing else to do."

"Oh, Lizard! Mary Ann!" It was Ginger, heading in our direction through the crowds of kids, waving frantically. "Come to the mall with us. We're all going together to get the big news!"

"Okay," Mary Ann said.

I shot her a look that said *I don't want to go with them*, but she ignored me.

"Fantastic!" Ginger said. "We're meeting outside. Luckily, it stopped raining."

We walked through the foyer and out the main entrance. I could hardly believe what I saw there. A mob of girls from my class—there must've been forty of them—crowding around, talking and laughing nervously.

"Are they *all* going to the mall?" I asked.

"You bet," Ginger said, planting herself next to Lisa. "We all sent in our head shots and bios, and we can't wait to see who was picked!" She waved her arm over her head as if she were signaling a wagon train to pull out. "Let's go!"

The girls gave one big squeal.

"Oh, I just can't believe it!" Tiffany gushed. "In about ten minutes, we'll all know!"

"I'm so scared, I don't want to look," Heather Parks said. "You look for me, Marcy. Tell me if my name's on the list. If it's not, don't say anything, just shake your head."

"Oh, boy." I looked at Mary Ann, and she gave me a wry smile. I knew she thought these girls were dumb, too, but she doesn't mind putting up with them the way I do.

"Just take it easy," Ginger said, putting her arm around Lisa's shoulders. "You know you'll get picked."

Lisa tossed her head and kept walking, but I could see she looked nervous.

The crowd got quiet as we approached the mall. Only anxious whispers and tiny, excited squeaks escaped from a couple of girls.

"I can hardly stand it," Ginger said. Then in a hushed voice, she added, "Let's hold hands."

The other girls took hands.

"No way," I said. "That's stupid."

"Oh, come on," Mary Ann whispered. "It's all part of the fun."

I folded my arms over my chest. Tiffany, next to me, turned and held out her hand. I shook my head. "No offense."

She shrugged and took Mary Ann's hand. Everyone moved in through the mall door, still holding hands. It hadn't occurred to anyone that it might be hard maneuvering through a door all connected like that, but they didn't let go of one another. They bumped the door with their butts and shoulders and passed it off to the person behind them. It was a strange thing to see, believe me.

Shoppers stopped to gawk as the mob moved through the mall.

"What's going on?" asked a woman about my grandma's age. I didn't know who she was talking to because she was standing alone.

"You wouldn't believe it if I told you," I said to her.

We rounded a corner, and one of the girls in front squealed, "There it is! On the wall by Pearson's!"

I stood on my toes and looked over the heads in the crowd. I couldn't see the list, but in front of it stood about thirty more girls, most of them older, craning their necks, shouting out names and whooping loudly.

The girls from my class broke hands and made a dash toward the group of older girls.

"Can you see it? Can you see any names?" Ginger cried over the noise.

Some of the older girls in front walked away, their shoulders drooping in disappointment. Others grinned and hugged each other, crying out, "Congratulations!"

"I can see Lisa's name!" shrieked Ginger.

"Lisa, you're on the list!"

Lisa closed her eyes and let out a huge breath. Then she nodded and smiled as if she'd known her name would be on the list all along.

"Okay, let's go home now," I said to Mary Ann.

"I want to see who else from our class was picked," she said.

"*Lizard Flanagan!*" Ginger screamed. "*Lizard Flanagan* is on the list! Oh, Lizard, *congratulations!* I didn't think you were interested in modeling."

A gasp went up around me, and people started thumping me on the back. "Congratulations!" they yelled in my ear.

"Lizard's on the list?" Lisa asked, her eyes wide.

"What are you talking about?" I said.

"You made the first cut!" Ginger smiled, but I could see disappointment in her eyes, too, because she wasn't on the list.

"That's impossible," I said. "I didn't apply."

"Well, somebody sent in your picture and bio," Ginger said. "And you were chosen."

I looked at Mary Ann. "Who would do a crummy thing like that? Did you?"

"No. Honest." She grinned. "I sent in *my* picture and bio, though."

"What? *You*? Why didn't you tell me?"

Mary Ann continued to smile. "What would you have said if I'd told you?"

"That you were nuts."

She laughed. "That's why I didn't tell you. But, Lizard, *you* were picked. Now, if you pass the interview, you'll be in the fashion show! Congratulations."

That's when the whole thing sank in. The fashion show!

"No way," I said. "I'm not even going to be in the audience."

"But if you're chosen after the interview," Mary Ann said, "you'll get fifty dollars for being in the show."

"Not in this lifetime," I said. "I don't care how much—" I stopped. "Wait a minute. What did you say?"

"Fifty dollars," Mary Ann said, grinning. "Just what you need to pay your parents back—*and* go to the Cubs game."

CHAPTER FOUR

THE GIRLS STOOD AROUND me in a tight clump, everybody talking at once.

"Lizard, you must be ecstatic!"

"What will you wear for your interview?"

"You going to cover up those scrapes with makeup?"

I nudged Mary Ann. "Let's get out of here."

She nodded, and we pushed through the crowd.

"See you tomorrow, Lizard!" Ginger called out and waved. "If I couldn't be picked, then I'm glad it was you!" Lisa gave her a sharp look. "After Lisa, I mean."

I headed for the door, pushed it open, and Mary Ann and I ran out into the damp air.

Mary Ann started laughing. "With all the girls who wanted to get picked so badly, you were the one chosen! I mean, you're pretty and all, but those girls work *hard* at being gorgeous! It's practically all they think about. You'd rather be outside playing baseball or something."

"Well, I'm not doing it."

"But, Lizard," she said, following after me, "you said you'd do anything to get the money to see the Cubs play."

"Anything but this," I said. "I feel the same way Wally did. I'd rather slay a dragon. I'd even rather get a lock of Wildwoman's hair."

"Being in a fashion show wouldn't be so bad," Mary Ann said. "All you'd have to do is walk around wearing different outfits."

"Forget it."

Mary Ann grinned slyly. "Wouldn't you like to go to Wrigley Field and eat hot dogs and watch Mark Grace play first base?"

That stopped me in my tracks. I blew out a breath. "Sure I would. You know I would."

"So go to the interview," she said. "If you pass it, you'll be in the fashion show. It'd be such an easy way to earn the money."

Just thinking about it made me nervous. "I can't, Mary Ann. I can't be up there in front of all those people."

"But—" A light of remembrance came into Mary Ann's eyes. "Oh, I get it now! It's because of what happened in fourth grade, right? You get stage fright."

"Yeah," I said. I was glad Mary Ann remembered. I didn't feel like talking about what happened on that horrible day.

We were giving oral reports about the early settlers. I started getting nervous a week ahead of time. I didn't sleep the night before. When it was my turn, Ms. Devon called my name, and I went up to the front of the room. My legs were trembling, and my mouth went dry. I started to give my report, and I got the hiccups. I hiccuped and hiccuped, and everybody laughed at me.

Ms. Devon told me to go down the hall and get a drink. I hurried down the hall and stopped right in front of the main entrance. *I could just run right out that door,* I thought. *I could go home and say I'd gotten sick and then* . . . But I realized I'd have to come back eventually and give my report. So I got a drink at the fountain and went back to the classroom. But the drink hadn't helped, and I hiccuped as I walked back into the room. The kids laughed even harder, and Ms. Devon told me just to hand in my written report. I got a C on it. Ever since then, I've refused to do *anything* in front of a crowd.

"But see?" Mary Ann said. "I'd forgotten about it, so I'm sure everyone else has, too. And that was two years ago. It won't happen again."

"How do you know?"

"You play ball," Mary Ann said. "You're the best pitcher our age for miles! See? Crowds don't bother you anymore."

"Playing ball is different," I said. "I'm concentrating on the game, and so are the fans. I don't have to say anything, and they don't care how I look. They just want to see the game."

We started walking again.

"You could go to the interview," suggested Mary Ann, "and just see what it's like. Would that make you nervous?"

"I don't think so, but what's the point? I'm not going to be in the fashion show."

"Do you know how many girls would give their right arm to be in it?"

"Would you?"

Mary Ann looked at the sidewalk and bit her lower lip the way she does when she feels uneasy. "Well, I wouldn't give my right arm." She looked up and grinned. "How could I play baseball without it? And I don't know if I really wanted to model in the fashion show so much. But I wanted to get picked. Do you know what I mean?"

"Yeah."

Mary Ann is a good friend. She's become a little more girly since elementary school, but I'm glad she still loves playing sports as much as she used to. And I understood what she meant about wanting to get picked. I had to admit it was flattering to be chosen.

"Who do you think sent in my picture and bio?" I asked her.

"I don't know. Did your mom know about the fashion show?"

"She never mentioned it. But I suppose it's possible. She liked it when I started braiding my hair—she kept telling me how nice it looked."

"Maybe she thought she'd surprise you," Mary Ann said.

"I hope she isn't too disappointed when I tell her I'm not going to the interview."

"I still think you should go," Mary Ann said. "I know it won't be as bad as you think.

And how else will you get the money to go to the Cubs game? It's the perfect solution!"

"No way."

It killed me to think of giving up a chance to see Mark Grace and Sammy Sosa play ball in person, but I was *not* going to model in a fashion show. And that was that.

I was sitting on the steps going up to the second floor when my mom got home from work. "Hi, Mom," I said as soon as she walked in the front door. She looked surprised, I guess, because I wasn't acting angry.

"Hi." She looked at me curiously, putting her big shoulder bag on the foyer table. "Have a good day?"

"Yeah. Hey, you didn't send in my picture for that fashion show thing, did you?"

"What fashion show thing?"

"At the Spring Pines Mall. Somebody sent in my picture and bio."

"No, I haven't heard anything about it. Why?"

"I was on the list of people picked to go on to the interview. The girls who pass the interview stage go on to the fashion show."

"Oh, Lizard." Mom's eyes lit up. "That's

wonderful! Congratulations."

"You didn't send in my picture?"

"No."

"You think Dad did?"

"I'm sure he would've told me if he had. Maybe Sam—"

"Are you kidding?"

Mom laughed. "On second thought, you're probably right."

Then it dawned on me. "Zach."

"You think Zach sent in your picture?"

"That's it! I gave him one of my school pictures."

I raced up the stairs to Mom's and Dad's room and dialed his number. He answered.

"Zach?"

"Hi."

"Did you send in my picture for that fashion show?"

There was a long pause. "Why?"

"I was picked to go to the interview," I told him.

I could hear him take in a breath. "You were?" Then he laughed. "That's great!"

"You sent in my picture, didn't you?"

"Yeah," he admitted.

"How come?"

"Well—I heard there was a fifty-dollar prize for everybody in the show."

"But I didn't even know about the trip to Chicago until yesterday."

"I know, but you always need money. You know, for baseball cards and stuff. And—well—" He paused. "Well, I thought you'd be good. You're not exactly ugly or anything."

I felt awkward suddenly. "Oh. Well, thanks."

Zach thinks I'm pretty. He didn't really say it, but that's what he meant.

"It'll be fun seeing you in the fashion show," he said. "And then with the money you'll get, you can come with us to the Cubs game."

That stopped me short. "Oh, well, I probably won't get picked for the show. I mean, there's an interview, and I hear it's really tough."

"You'll do okay."

I felt guilty that he'd sent in my picture and bio, and I wasn't even planning on going to the interview! I didn't have the heart to tell him, either. I also didn't want to tell him about my stage fright, which is really embarrassing. I'd have to figure out a way to tell him. Just not now. He seemed so happy for me.

You'd think I'd single-handedly won the World Series, the way everyone was acting at school the next day.

"Hi, gorgeous model!" Ginger sang out at our locker in the morning. Lisa stood next to her, her weight over one hip, looking at me critically.

I rolled my eyes. "Ginger, don't call me that, okay?"

"Why not?" Ginger's voice gets shrill when she's excited, and her voice screeched through the hall. "The judges think you're model material. Just think, here I am, standing with the two girls from our class who were chosen to go on to the interview. I'm so lucky!"

"Yeah, right." Then I added, smiling just a little, "But, hey, I wouldn't mind a little bowing and scraping. In fact, after school you could clean out my closets and paint my room, then order me a big double-cheese pizza."

The second the joke was out of my mouth, I was sorry.

Ginger sank to her knees, held her arms

over her head and bowed till her forehead was on the floor. "Oh, hail, models from my class! I'm at your service. Anything you desire, I'll try and get for you."

I glanced around, feeling my face heat up like a furnace. "Geez, get up, Ginger. That was a *joke*," I told her. "Come on, people are staring at us."

Lisa just watched her, chomping on a big wad of gum. She didn't look embarrassed at all.

Heather and Tiffany came over and slapped Lisa and me on the back. Ginger finally got up off the floor.

"Congratulations," Heather said. "I hate you both." She made it sound as if it was a joke, but I think she meant it.

"I hate you, too," Tiffany said. "Ha-ha. No really, I'm happy for you guys."

"Did you find out who sent in your picture and bio?" Ginger asked me.

"Yeah," I told her. "It was Zach."

"Zach?" Lisa said in disbelief.

Ginger's mouth popped open. "Ohhhh," she gushed, "how fantastically romantic!" She looked around at Lisa, Heather, and Tiffany. "Have you ever heard of anything so sweet?

Zach has such a thoughtful, caring personality. Plus, let's not forget, a great bod."

"He's one in a million," Heather agreed.

"He sure is," Tiffany said.

Lisa sniffed. "If you like the type."

Ginger laughed. "You sure *used* to." Lisa glared daggers at her.

That was pretty funny. Lisa and Zach had gone out together for a couple of weeks, but he dumped her when he realized what a jerk she was. Ever since then, she'd been acting as if *she* dumped *him*.

"No offense, Lizard," Lisa said, "but I wouldn't count on being in the fashion show. Those scrapes on your face will count against you. Models are supposed to be flawless."

That gave me an idea. But I plastered a disappointed look on my face and said, "Maybe you're right."

"What are you going to wear to the interview?" Lisa asked me. Her gaze traveled down my T-shirt and jeans to my running shoes and back up again. She smiled smugly. "Do you have any nice clothes?"

"I don't know what I'll wear," I said, the idea blossoming in my mind. I was beginning to feel better every second.

"Well, you'll need to start shopping," Lisa said. "The interview is Friday."

Ginger squealed. "This is so exciting! Why don't we all come with you after school today, Lizard? We can help you find just the right outfit to impress the interviewer."

"Uh, no, thanks," I said, backing away. "I can take care of that myself." I turned and hurried away.

I couldn't imagine shopping with those girls. I'm not into self-torture.

P.E. is my favorite class by far. It's the only subject in which I know for sure I'll get an A, no matter what. The only part I hate is taking showers. What a way to ruin a fun class!

I was one of the first to get to the girls' locker room. I changed into my gym clothes and went into the gym and sat on the bleachers to wait. The gym was empty except for me.

"I just can't believe Lizard Flanagan was picked!"

I heard the voice coming from around the corner leading to the girls' locker room. It sounded a lot like Lisa.

"I know. She's cute, but there are *hundreds* of girls who are as pretty as she is." That was definitely Tiffany.

"She'll never make it past the interview," Lisa said. "She's all scraped up, and she walks like a jock. That's enough to keep her out right there." She laughed. "But that body! They'll take one look at that stick body of hers and say, 'Don't call us, we'll call you!'"

They laughed, and their voices faded into the locker room.

My heart slammed against my ribs and adrenaline shot through my body. How dare they talk about me behind my back that way! They wouldn't have the nerve to say it to my face. They knew I'd knock them both into the next county.

I'd been chosen fair and square, just the way Lisa was. I deserved to go to the interview! So what if I was thin? I was physically fit, and I'd seen plenty of models who aren't well developed. I'd show them!

Wait a minute, I thought. *I don't want to get chosen! I'd get the hiccups for sure, or trip and fall on my face, or throw up before the show because I was so nervous.*

I'd have to stick to my plan.

But the inside of my chest still burned with hatred for Lisa and Tiffany.

When everyone was out on the gym floor and Mrs. Puff had taken roll, she announced that we were going to play softball with the boys again. We'd been in a softball unit since school started, which was fine with me. Softball is one of my specialties.

Outside on the diamond, Mrs. Puff and Mr. Groden made Nathan Morgan and me captains.

I won the coin toss and got to pick first. My choice was Ed Mechtensteimer, out of loyalty. He's a good player, but not the best. Tom Luther is the best, just after me. That sounds like a brag, but it's a stone cold fact. Anyway, Tom had a six hundred batting average in our metro league. I figured Morgan's first pick would be Luther, and it was.

Morgan and I took turns choosing teammates. I chose Mike Herman and a few other good guys. I didn't want to pick Stinky because I was still ticked off at him for making comments about my body. But he's a better player than the people who were left after most of the others had been picked, and the game was the important thing. So he ended up on my team. Morgan picked Andy Walinsky, Brad Williams, Sara Pulliam, and Jennifer Peterson. I picked Ginger almost last, and just so I wouldn't have to pick Lisa or Tiffany. Ginger jumped up and down and squealed as if she'd been my first choice.

Lisa rolled her eyes at Tiffany and tossed her hair over her shoulder.

Ed and I decided that I should pitch, he would play first base, Stinky second. Mike Herman would play shortstop.

First up at bat was Nathan Morgan. He stepped into the box and grinned at me. He knew I wouldn't be easy on him.

"Show him what you've got," Ed called. I saw him glance over at Sara Pulliam. He was probably hoping to impress her with his playing.

My first pitch was a little high, and Morgan wasn't expecting it. He swung, and missed. The second pitch, another fastball, he hit to the outfield. Then he streaked to first base.

"Yea, Nathan!" Tiffany hollered from the batting line.

Next up was Tom Luther. He screwed up his face the way he always does when he's really concentrating and stared at me, waiting for the pitch.

I wound up and threw him my curveball. Luther connected and slammed it high into the air. He ran for first base, but before he was halfway there we could see the ball curve into a foul. He walked back to the box and tried again, closing his stance a little. His face was so determined, so tense, I almost laughed. *He's as competitive as I am*, I thought.

I wasn't going to make it easy for him. I served up my fastball, and he hit a grounder to Mike Herman at shortstop. Mike snared it and fired it to Stinky on second. Stinky shot it to Mechtensteimer on first.

I leaped in the air and shouted, "Great double play, guys!"

"Fantastic double play!" Ginger whooped and danced in a circle out in left field. "What an amazing double play! Hey, Lizard?"

"Yeah?"

"A double play is when you get two guys out, right in a row?" I nodded. She nodded back. "Great double play, guys!" She gave them a thumbs-up.

Mechtensteimer laughed and shook his head at me. I grinned. At least Ginger was learning. Lisa and Tiffany couldn't have cared less what a double play was.

Next up was none other than Lisa St. George. I couldn't wait to strike her out.

She hauled the bat up over her shoulder and glared at me. I smiled back, and she frowned harder. "What're you grinning at?" she asked.

"You want to play ball?" I asked her.

"Isn't that what we're doing?" she snapped.

"Then step into the batter's box, why don't you? Look where you're standing."

She looked down and saw that she was a foot closer to me than she should've been. She rolled her eyes, huffed loudly, and said, "Big deal." She stepped back into the batter's box and glared at me. "You going to throw that stupid ball or what?"

Oh, was I ever.

I wound up and fired my fastball. It was right down the middle, but she yelped and leaped backward. "You tried to hit me!" she shrieked.

"Strike one!"

"Lisa," I said, "I didn't try to hit you. If I'd wanted to hit you, I would have." *Right between the eyes.*

"You wanted to mess up my face so I wouldn't be chosen for the fashion show!"

"*What?*"

"You're trying to keep me out of the fashion show!"

I didn't know what to say. How do you argue with a prima donna who thinks she's the center of the universe?

"Come on, Lisa," Luther complained from the back of the line. "Just swing, will you? We want to play ball."

To be funny, I bowed to her, then threw her a slow, underhand pitch. She swung too soon and missed it by miles. The guys all roared.

"Strike two!" Mechtensteimer hollered. "And, Lisa, that was about as polite as Lizard gets."

"Very funny, Lizard," she said.

"Here's your last pitch." I threw her my curve down the middle, and by some magic bit of luck, she swung and hit it. She stood there a second as if she couldn't believe it. The ball dribbled up the middle of the field.

"Run!" Morgan and Luther yelled at her.

I have to admit that I was just as surprised as she was. But I recovered the ball and threw it to Mechtensteimer on first. Ed grabbed it and tagged the base before Lisa got there. Now we were up at bat.

Ed stepped up to the batter's box.

"Eddie, Eddie. He's our man. If he can't do it, no one can!" Ginger shouted, and she rocked her hips back and forth.

I turned to her. "You want to keep it down, Ginger? Let him concentrate."

"Oh, sure. No problem."

Morgan served up a fastball, and Ed swung. He hit a long, high drive to center field, which I'm sure impressed the heck out of Sara. Tiffany, who was right under it, held up her hands. "I got it, I got it," she said.

The ball landed in her glove and bounced out onto the ground. She frowned. "The darned thing just jumped out of my hands."

"Throw it here!" Luther shouted from first base.

Tiffany watched Ed reach first base, then shrugged. "Too late."

I tried to stifle a laugh. Was I glad Lisa and Tiffany weren't on my team!

I was up next.

"Get her out, Nathan!" Lisa shouted from right field.

Nathan wound up and threw me a curve.

Crack! I fired it right to Lisa. If the Guinness Book of World Records had a spot for worst catcher, Lisa would have had it sewn up. As I ran to first base, I looked up to see Lisa do a little prancing step toward it. But when she saw it catapulting down toward her, she stepped back and let it plop on the ground at her feet.

I'd already arrived at first base.

"Why didn't you catch it?" Mike Herman yelled at Lisa.

"If you must know, I have to protect my nails for the fashion show interview."

The whole game was like that. We steam-rolled Morgan's team as easy as you please. The victory was sweet, but not as sweet as it would've been if we'd actually had some competition. The final score at the end of the period was 13–3.

I was feeling awfully good until I realized it was time for showers. We'd been showering in front of each other for a couple of weeks, so we were getting used to it. But as soon as I had my clothes off, I looked up to see Lisa watching me. She turned to Tiffany and Heather and whispered loudly enough so that I could hear, "As soon as the interviewer sees that tomboy body, she's out for sure."

"She's built like a pencil. A *strong* pencil, but still a pencil," Tiffany whispered back.

They laughed.

The other girls heard them, too, and smiled.

My face must have turned a dozen shades of red. I gritted my teeth and stalked past them to Mrs. Puff, who stood next to the shower with her clipboard. "Flanagan," I said to her, so she could check me off the shower list.

I think I only got my hands wet, but I don't remember exactly. I was so angry and embarrassed that I couldn't think straight. Mrs. Puff didn't seem to notice that I spent about five seconds in the shower before I hurried back to get dressed.

I was out of the locker room in a minute. I stalked down the hall, furious.

I hated Lisa and Heather and Tiffany with a white-hot passion. If only I could have a minute in a boxing ring with them. I could whip them all at once with one arm tied behind my back!

Oh, why did Zach have to send in my picture?

There was no way I was going to model in that fashion show! The last thing I wanted to do was walk around in front of hundreds of people, a lot of them probably like Lisa and Tiffany and Heather. They'd all be watching me and whispering about my body, and then I'd get the hiccups and humiliate myself.

Not even the Cubs were worth that!

My stomach felt horrible. Seeing the Cubs play in person had been my lifetime dream. I'd thought a hundred times about catching a fly ball or getting Mark Grace's autograph or just sitting in the stands, eating a Wrigley Field hot dog and cheering on my favorite team.

Now, finally, I had a chance to make my dream come true. And I was going to miss it.

CHAPTER FIVE

OVER THE NEXT TWO days I perfected my plan for the interview. It was scheduled for four-thirty Friday afternoon.

Friday morning I met Mary Ann at the bridge over the ravine. "I'm glad you decided to go to the interview," she said.

"Yeah." I hadn't let her in on my plan. I figured she'd try to talk me out of it, and I was determined that nothing would stop me from putting my plan into action. Still, I felt guilty that I hadn't told her.

"I bet it won't be bad at all," she said. "And, with a little luck, before you know it we'll be on that bus heading for Wrigley Field." She grinned. "Al called me last night. He says he'll probably go, too."

I tried to smile. "Great." Mary Ann really

Al, but I wondered if she'd go to the game without me. I felt guilty again. Mary Ann was daydreaming about the thinking I'd be there, too.

ven if you're nervous at the interview," Ann said, "try to act cool. Sit and cross your legs and don't fidget. And be sure to shake the hand of the interviewer." She smiled again. "I read an article about how to get into teen modeling yesterday while I waited in the checkout line at Whetstone's," she explained. "Come on, let's go."

I pedaled toward school behind Mary Ann. I didn't feel much like talking. It was so depressing, giving up a chance to see the Cubs in person. But what else could I do? There was no way I could be in a fashion show.

The morning dragged by. At lunch, Zach seemed awfully quiet.

"Hey, Walters," Stinky said with a big grin on his face. "I heard about the play you're in."

Zach nodded and swallowed a bite of hamburger casserole.

"What play?" I asked.

"It's not a play," Zach said.

Stinky shrugged. "Well, okay, a scene from a play." He turned to me. "Mrs. Brown's language arts classes are studying plays, so they're going to put on three scenes from melodramas. They'll have to memorize lines and everything." He smiled slyly. "Zach's going to be Count Dracula. He spends half the scene in a coffin."

Ed grinned. "Cool."

Andy Walinsky said, "Yeah, I heard about that. Cassandra March is in the scene too."

Ed's eyes widened. "Cassandra March? That's *really* cool."

Cassandra is one of the cutest girls in our class. Not drop-dead gorgeous like Lisa St. George, but very pretty. And I'd heard she was nice. Everybody seemed to like her.

"Yeah, but you haven't heard the best part," Stinky said. "In the scene, Zach has to climb out of the coffin, sneak up behind Cassandra and bite her neck!"

"Wow," Ed said, his eyes as big as the plates on the table. "I'd like to get that close to Cassandra March."

"I bet Sara Pulliam would find that very interesting," I said, "seeing as how you're supposed to be going out with her."

Ed's face darkened. "You'd better not tell her, Lizard."

"Maybe I will, and maybe I won't."

I'd never tell her what Ed said, but it was fun teasing him. Besides, he shouldn't drool over Cassandra when he's going out with Sara.

Zach didn't say much. In fact, he didn't even seem to be paying attention to the conversation. I figured he must be embarrassed by how the guys were needling him. I was glad he didn't act goofy about biting Cassandra's neck, the way they did.

After school, I found Ginger standing next to our locker, waiting for me.

"Your interview is at Jackson's Department Store at four-thirty, right?" she said.

"Yeah."

"You want Tiff and Heather and me to come to the interview with you? I mean, we wouldn't go *into* the interview with you— unless you want us to."

What a horrible thought. "No, thanks," I said.

"We're going with Lisa at four forty-five, but we could go earlier with you to give you moral support—you know, talk with you and keep you pumped while you wait your turn. And then, while you're interviewing, we'll wait with Lisa and help her stay calm." Ginger laughed. "It's funny that you'll probably need pumping up, and Lisa'll need calming down. See? Friends just know these things. We can help at important times like these."

"Thanks anyway."

"Isn't Mary Ann going with you?" Ginger asked.

"Nope."

"Whew. You sure are brave."

"Well, I have to go get ready now. Mary Ann's waiting outside to ride home with me."

"Oh, sure," Ginger said. "Now remember, be peppy. Models should be like cheerleaders, real happy and perky."

"Perky?"

"Yeah. You know, bubbly and stuff."

"Oh, sure."

The article that Mary Ann read had said just the opposite. Sit quietly, cross your legs, and shake the interviewer's hand.

I met Mary Ann outside by the bike rack, as we'd planned, and we headed home.

"So what did you decide to wear to your interview?" Mary Ann asked.

"Oh—well, maybe my denim skirt. I don't know."

Mary Ann's mouth dropped open. "You mean, you haven't decided yet? But your interview is in less than an hour!"

"Well—" I was tempted to tell Mary Ann about my plan, but I was sure she'd try to talk me out of it, and I didn't have time for that. Besides, I didn't want her to start reminding me that I wouldn't be going to the Cubs game. I felt bad enough about it already, but I just had to do it this way. "Yeah, I'll probably wear my denim skirt," I said.

"Oh," she said. "That'll look nice."

When we got to the bridge over the ravine, she called, "Good luck!"

"Thanks," I said.

I rode home and went straight up to my room. I got out what I'd really planned to wear to the interview: a pair of jeans with tears just above the knees, a sweatshirt that said I'M A CUBS FANATIC! and my favorite pair of sneakers. I didn't fix my hair, but left the wisps that had pulled out of my braid hanging loose around my face. Then the crowning touch: I put my Chicago Cubs cap on backward. I looked in the mirror.

The effect was great, especially with the scratches on my chin. Lisa said models are supposed to be flawless, and that definitely did not describe me. I grinned at my reflection. I'd never make it past the interview.

I hopped on my bike and rode to the Spring Pines Mall. Part of me was feeling great. After all, I wouldn't have to model in that dumb fashion show. But the rest of me was feeling sad because I'd miss sitting with my best buddies at Wrigley Field, watching my heroes play ball.

I locked my bike to a small tree near Jackson's and walked inside. I figured the interviews would be held in the offices, so I took the escalator to the second floor.

At the customer service desk sat a woman with lots of eye makeup and fire-engine-red fingernails. She would've looked very sophisticated, but she was chewing a wad of gum, and that sort of ruined the effect.

"Hi," I said. "Could you tell me where the fashion show interviews are being held?"

She looked me up and down. "You're interviewing?"

"Yes. I'm Lizard Flanagan."

She riffled through some papers and ran

her fingers down a list of names. Then she glanced at the clock on the wall that said it was four twenty-five. "Have a seat," she said. "Ms. Landers will be with you in a few minutes."

"Thanks."

I plopped into a chair next to the wall. The woman with the gum kept looking up at me from her paperwork, but I pretended not to notice. Mary Ann said I should cross my legs at the knee and be poised, so I swung my legs back and forth under my chair.

After a few minutes, a door opened and an older girl walked out. She was very dressed up, and she was beautiful—a sixteen-year-old version of Lisa. She turned to someone still inside the office.

"Thanks, Ms. Landers," she said, smiling with perfect, blinding-white teeth. "It was nice to meet you."

She was like a walking, talking Barbie doll.

She glanced curiously at me, then left, walking smoothly on mile-high heels.

In a moment, a pretty woman in a blue suit came to the door. "Lizard?"

"Yeah?" I stood up.

Her eyes took me in swiftly. "Come in."

I followed her into the office. "Have a seat," she said.

I sat in the plastic chair next to her desk.

"Congratulations on making the preliminary list," she said.

"Thanks." I rested my ankle over the opposite knee.

"Your name is Lizard?" She smiled. "That's unusual."

I shrugged and grinned. "Yeah, I know. It's really Elizabeth, but my twin brother couldn't say that when we were little. It came out sounding like Lizard, and it stuck. I like it better than Elizabeth."

Ms. Landers smiled again and looked at the paper in front of her. "I see you like sports."

"Yes," I said. "I love baseball."

"Are you a spectator or a player?"

"Both."

"What position do you play?"

"I pitch."

Ms. Landers's smile widened. "Good for you. My husband used to play major-league ball."

I sat up with interest and put my foot

82

down. "You're kidding. Who with?"

"St. Louis. Just for a couple of seasons."

"What position?"

"Catcher. He was pretty good. When our daughter was born, though, he decided he'd better get into something more stable. He sells insurance now."

"So does my dad."

"Where?"

"At the Perkins Agency," I said.

"Small world. So does Mike."

"Oh, yeah," I said, grinning. "I've heard my dad talk about Mike Landers. I hear he's a great bowler."

Ms. Landers laughed. "He sure is." She gazed at me thoughtfully for a moment. "Lizard, take off the cap, please."

I did.

"Stand up, will you?"

I stood.

"Walk over to the window, turn around and come back. But don't sit until I say so."

That sounded easy. I did what she asked.

"You're not like the others who've come to interview," she said. "You probably already know that."

I put on a surprised look. "I'm not?"

Ms. Landers just smiled. "You may sit down. What else do you like to do, besides play baseball?"

"Well, I like football and riding my bike and fishing and camping and catching frogs—"

"I get the picture," Ms. Landers said. "Are you treating those scrapes with anything?"

"Well, I wash them in the shower."

"Try an antibiotic cream," she said. "They'll heal faster."

I shrugged. "Okay."

"If you were selected for the show," Ms. Landers said, "would you be able to practice every night for two weeks?"

"I s'ppose."

"How are your grades?"

"Mostly Bs. The rest As."

"What's your favorite subject in school?" I opened my mouth to answer, and she added, "Besides P.E."

"Oh. Well, I guess it would be lunch."

Ms. Landers laughed. "What would you like to be when you grow up?"

"I haven't really thought about it," I said seriously. "I'm only twelve."

"Well, I'll say one thing, Lizard," Ms.

Landers said, "you're a refreshing change. The other girls all say they want to be either doctors or models."

I made a face. "Yuck."

She laughed again. "I'm surprised you mailed in an application for the show."

"I didn't," I said. "A friend of mine did."

"Was it a joke?"

"No. He thought I'd be good."

She smiled. "Well, I'll be calling everyone tonight to let them know my decisions."

I stood up. "Okay. Thanks." On an impulse, I stuck out my hand. "'Bye, Ms. Landers."

She shook my hand. "Good-bye, Lizard. Thanks for coming in."

"Sure."

I walked out of the office, and standing there were Lisa, Ginger, Tiffany, and Heather. They were all dressed up, especially Lisa, who wore an outfit so fancy, I'd only consider wearing it for the presidential inauguration if my dad were elected.

They all gawked at my outfit, and I grinned.

"Hi, guys," I said. "Have fun. Ms. Landers is really cool." I left before they recovered from their shock.

I rode my bike home knowing I'd accomplished my goal. Even though Ms. Landers seemed surprised at how I was dressed, she was still nice. But there was no way she'd pick me to model.

Even though she'd said I was "refreshing," I could tell she meant refreshing with a tinge of weird. And when she said the others wanted to be doctors or models, I'd said "Yuck." It had just popped out, but it was the perfect thing to say. I'd played it just right.

As I rode up my front sidewalk, though, a sinking feeling crept into my stomach. I was glad I wouldn't be modeling in the fashion show, but it meant that I'd miss out on all the fun at Wrigley Field. Still, even seeing the Cubs play wouldn't be worth getting up on stage in front of all those people. That would be a nightmare!

I knew I'd done the right thing. I just wished I felt better about it.

CHAPTER SIX

"**I WENT TO THE INTERVIEW** this afternoon."

Zach passed the football to me, and I ran toward the evergreens at the end of the yard to catch it. Klondike, Zach's dog, stood next to the garage and barked.

"How'd it go?" he asked.

"Fine." I fired the ball back to him. It brushed his fingertips and bounced at his feet. Klondike bounded over to it, but Zach snatched it out of his way.

"I don't think I'll get picked, though," I said. "I saw some of the other girls. They were really beautiful."

"Uh-huh." He passed the football back.

Zach seemed very distracted. He missed an easy catch, and he threw me a couple of wimpy passes that were miles below his usual standards.

"Your mom make anything good for dessert tonight?" I asked.

I had been hoping he'd offer me some, the way he usually did. But since he hadn't, I took the direct approach.

"Oh, yeah. Apple pie. You want some?"

"Sure."

I'm very deprived in the dessert department. My mom never makes them, on general principle, and dad doesn't usually have the time. So I come over to Zach's to satisfy my sweet tooth.

Inside, Zach cut me a piece of pie. "Frozen yogurt on top?"

"What kind?"

Zach opened the big freezer, leaned over, and peered into the basket on the bottom. "Vanilla, caramel, or brownie fudge?"

"Vanilla," I said. "But I'll do it."

I pulled the ice-cream scoop from the kitchen drawer and dug a big chunk out of the hard yogurt.

"Your mom is the best baker in the world." I plopped the yogurt on top. "You want some?"

"Yeah."

I scooped out a big ball of yogurt for him

and put it on his pie. We went out and sat on the back porch. Klondike sat alert at our feet, hoping for a handout. We always let him lick our plates, so he had a hurry-up-and-finish-it look in his eyes.

"Cool it, Klondike," I said. "I'm going to enjoy this pie no matter how pathetic you look."

Klondike whimpered, then jumped around and landed at my feet, barking.

"He misunderstood you," Zach said. "He thought you said, 'Get ready, Klondike. I hope you enjoy this pie I'm going to throw to you.'"

I laughed. We ate till we were stuffed. Then we put our plates on the patio so Klondike could lick off the melted yogurt that was left.

"When Sam and I were younger, we had this great baby-sitter who baked for us. She'd make cakes and pies and cookies all the time."

"Sounds better than the baby-sitter I had," Zach said. "Mrs. Barnhart used to lock me in the closet when she got tired of me."

I grinned. I loved Zach's stories. "So what happened?"

Zach leaned forward, his elbows on his knees. "Well, I finally got my revenge. One time, after she shut the door, I ran my hand over the closet wall and felt a button I hadn't known was there. I pushed it, and a door popped open in the wall behind me."

"What was on the other side?"

"A hidden staircase," Zach said. "I was careful to lock the secret door behind me so Mrs. Barnhart couldn't follow me if she found it. I tiptoed down the steps and into a basement room that I didn't know existed. It was filled with spy equipment: a pen that was really a tiny camera, special computers that decode secret messages, fingerprint-dusting kits, things like that."

"Cool."

"I'd suspected for a long time that my dad was a secret agent, but this proved it. I had a hunch that Mrs. Barnhart was a foreign spy, and she was posing as a baby-sitter so she could snoop around the house."

"What did you do?"

"I found a door leading into the main part of the basement," he said. "I sneaked up-stairs and peeked at Mrs. Barnhart. She was taking pictures of some papers on my dad's desk. So I took pictures of her with the pen camera. I picked up a glass she'd been using to guzzle our supply of Diet Coke and dusted it for fingerprints. Then I set up a trap."

"How'd you do that?"

"I wrote a note using my dad's handwriting that said the CIA papers on the Underwood Project were hidden in the coat closet."

"What was the Underwood Project?"

"I just made it up. It sounded official and like something Barnhart would be nosy about."

"Did she go for it?"

He nodded. "Like Klondike to your dessert plate. She rushed to the closet. And a second later, she was my prisoner in that cramped, dark place. My dad turned her in and proved with the evidence I'd collected that she was a foreign spy. She's in prison right now, chained to a concrete wall in her cell."

"All right!"

Zach leaned back on the porch railing. "I hated that closet."

Mary Ann jogged around the side of the house. "Lizard, I'm so glad I found you!" she said. "Hi, Zach." Her face was flushed, and she looked really excited. She stopped and breathed heavily. She must've run from her house.

"What's up?" I asked.

"Great news, Lizard! The best!"

Inside my stomach, it suddenly felt as if a little man was stomping around on the apple pie and yogurt.

"What?" I said. "What happened?"

Stomp, stomp, stomp, stomp.

"I was just at your house looking for you," she said, grinning. "The phone rang, and your mom told me that it was the woman who interviewed you for the fashion show."

Oh, no. Not that. If Mary Ann was happy about it, this wasn't a good sign! The stomping got worse.

STOMP, STOMP, STOMP, STOMP.

I didn't want to hear the answer, but I asked anyway. "What did she say?" I braced myself.

Mary Ann beamed. "Congratulations! You got in! You were picked for the Spring Pines fashion show! Isn't that wonderful?"

The little man in my stomach ran up into my throat and back down and punched my heart a few times for good measure.

"Wow! Way to go, Lizard!" Zach grinned

and clapped me on the back. "I knew you'd be good."

"But how could I have— How could she have wanted me—" I stopped. "I don't get it."

"She saw model material in you, dummy!" Mary Ann said, laughing. "Now we can all go to Wrigley Field and see the Cubs play!"

"The fashion show will be great," Zach said. "All the guys'll come. We'll be there in the crowd rooting for you. You'll show that stuck-up Lisa a thing or two."

I realized my mouth was hanging open, so I closed it. That man was still hopping up and down in my stomach, and I thought I might lose the pie I'd just eaten.

"Oh, Lizard, this is so exciting!" Mary Ann said.

"I have to go home now."

"How come?" Zach asked.

Mary Ann smiled, understanding. "You'll be fine, Lizard."

"I—uh, I have to do my homework. See you."

I hurried out of Zach's backyard and headed for home.

How could this have happened? I went to the interview looking crummy, with messy hair. I crossed my ankle over my knee and talked about baseball! How could I have failed to make Ms. Landers think I'd be a terrible model?

Oh, this was horrible! I felt sick.

I'd have to think of a way to get out of the fashion show. I couldn't walk around in front of all those people while they stared at me.

I'd rather die!

CHAPTER SEVEN

"**YOU DID IT!**" **GINGER** screeched when I arrived at school with Mary Ann on Monday. Kids were piling off the buses in front of Truman. "You're going to be in the fashion show with Lisa!"

She ran over to me, followed by Lisa, Tiffany, and Heather. "I heard it from Lisa, who heard it from Sara Pulliam, who heard it from Mary Ann."

I glanced at Mary Ann. "Thanks a lot."

"We're all excited for you, Lizard," Mary Ann said. Then she lowered her voice and leaned in so the others couldn't hear. "This'll be a good chance for you to conquer your fear. You'll just be showing off some outfits."

Ginger stepped closer. "What'd you say, Mary Ann?"

Mary Ann turned back to her. "I just said we're all so proud of Lizard." Lisa glowered at her. "And Lisa, too!"

Some other kids saw Lisa and me and came over to stare at us as if we were celebrities or something.

"I just can't believe it!" Ginger said. "Two of my best friends are going to be models! And one of you just might win the Supermodel prize!" She whipped a camera out of her book bag and snapped a picture of me. "Just think, you could become rich supermodels someday! Maybe you'll even get on that show that comes into your mansion and looks at how glamorous everything is. Okay, now I want to get a picture of you guys on the first day of your lives as famous models! Come on, Lisa and Lizard. Stand next to each other, you two."

More kids crowded around us now.

I didn't move. "I don't want my picture taken, Ginger."

"Well, you'd better get used to it, girl! You're going to be getting your picture taken a lot if you're going into modeling!"

"I'm not going into modeling," I told her. In fact, I was still trying to figure out a way to get out of the fashion show. Money or no money—this just wasn't worth it.

"Lisa, stand next to Lizard," Ginger directed, waving her hand.

Lisa sighed loudly and came over and stood next to me.

"Put your arms around each other," Ginger instructed. "This is the happiest day of your lives, getting into the exciting world of fashion modeling!"

It would be a cold day in July before I'd put my arm around that snot Lisa. But she plastered a fake smile on her face and put her arm around my shoulder. Ginger snapped the picture.

"Perfect!" Ginger said. "But, Lizard, models are supposed to smile when the photographer asks them to."

I grabbed Mary Ann's arm and dragged her through the crowd.

"This is ridiculous," I said, stalking away. "Now I know how the animals at the zoo feel, with everybody gawking at them."

"It'll die down," Mary Ann said, smiling. "It's just new. Everyone wants to see you and be a part of the excitement."

"What excitement?" I said. "I hate this!"

I led her behind a lilac bush. "I have to get out of the fashion show."

"But, Lizard, you'll do a great job! It won't be like in fourth grade because you won't have to say anything! You'll just walk around in different outfits."

I looked right at Mary Ann. "I tried to sabotage my interview," I confessed. I told her what I'd worn, and as I talked, her eyes got as big as baseballs. "I did everything wrong! I crossed my ankle over my knee and talked about pitching! I was *sure* she'd never pick me."

"Wow," Mary Ann said. "How come you didn't tell me you were going to do that?"

"I knew you'd try to talk me out of it."

Mary Ann laughed. "Just like you would've done if I'd told you I was sending in my picture and bio."

"Yeah," I said.

"I knew you didn't want to be in the fashion show," Mary Ann said, "but you really worked at not getting chosen! But what about the Cubs game? You want to—"

"Nothing is worth having to get up in front of all those people!"

Mary Ann smiled again. "All that, and she

picked you, anyway. You must've done something right!"

"Ms. Landers told me her husband used to play for St. Louis, and we had a good conversation—"

"That's it!" Mary Ann said.

"What?"

"The article I read said the most important thing is to be yourself and establish a relationship with the interviewer."

"That's what I did," I said miserably.

"And she loved you! You didn't give me a chance to tell you last night that she said you were a breath of fresh air."

"Boy, did I ever louse things up. I don't know how I'm going to get out of this."

"You're not."

"Mary Ann, I can't—"

"Yes, you can! You're going to model in the fashion show, and you're going to be *good*."

"No, I'm not—"

"And then after the show, we'll get on the bus and ride to Wrigley Field to see the Cubs play *in person*."

I sighed. "Boy, I'd love to see the Cubbies play."

"You will. You can do it, Lizard. Just keep saying, 'I'm going to see the Cubbies. I'm going to see the Cubbies.' Concentrate on how much fun the trip will be."

"Why do you think I'd be good?" I asked her. "You know what happened in fourth grade with the hiccups."

"That was two whole years ago! You're mature now. You can handle it."

"You think two years can make a difference?"

"Of course," Mary Ann said. "Look, isn't tonight the first rehearsal for the fashion show?"

"Yeah."

"Go and see what it's like. All you do is wear a couple of outfits and walk around. How hard can that be?"

I sighed. "I guess I can go to the rehearsal tonight. But I won't promise to be in the show."

Mary Ann grinned. "Okay."

The bell rang, and everyone headed toward the building.

"Don't you have to be at your fashion show rehearsal at six-thirty?" Mom said, stopping in the doorway of my room.

"Yeah." I was sorting through my baseball card collection.

"We'd better go. You don't want to be late." She smiled. "This is really exciting, Lizard. I can't wait to see you in the show."

I put down my cards and stared at her. "You're planning to come to the fashion show?"

She frowned. "Of course!"

"Is Dad coming too?"

"Sure, and so is Sam. Grandma's even planning to drive down to see you."

Good grief. My whole family would see me humiliate myself.

Mom dropped me outside the main entrance to the mall. I went inside and down the escalator to the basement floor. We were practicing where Stevenson's men's store used to be, because it was still empty. I rounded the corner and saw Ginger, Tiffany, and Heather standing in front of Stevenson's. The new front was under construction, and there was white paper over the glass front, so you couldn't see inside the store.

"We thought you weren't coming!" Ginger squealed. She ran over to me.

"What are you guys doing here?" I said.

"We came with Lisa, and we were worried when you didn't show up."

I checked my watch. "I'm five minutes early."

"Really?" Ginger said. "We thought maybe you'd forgotten about it."

"Well, I didn't, so you can stop worrying and go home now."

"Lisa didn't think she needed us to stay," Ginger said, "but we could wait here for you, if you want. You'll probably have breaks, and we can keep you energized."

"Thanks anyway."

"Well, okay," Ginger said. "But memorize every detail so you can tell us what happened."

"I'm sure Lisa will tell you all about it."

"But that'll just be her side of things," Ginger said. "We want to hear about it from you, too."

"Sure."

"Well, have a fantastic time!" Ginger said. She didn't move. "We'll wait till you get inside."

I rolled my eyes. "See you."

I went into the store. A circle of sixteen chairs stood in the middle of the floor, facing the center. Most of the chairs were already filled. Girls my age and older sat in the circle. Ms. Landers stooped over a table at the side of the room, looking at a large notebook. She glanced up at me.

"Hi, Lizard. Come and get a name tag."

When I walked across the room to the table, the other girls looked me up and down critically. It reminded me of the way my dad looks over a side of beef at the locker before he buys it. I guess they were wondering if I'd be competition for that hundred-dollar Supermodel prize.

I picked up my name tag, put it on, and sat down in the closest empty chair. Next to me was an older girl with long, dark, wavy hair and eyebrows that looked crayoned onto her face.

"Hi," she said. She squinted at my tag. "Lizard? That's an unusual name."

"I know."

Her tag said ABBY BOWEN. She wiped her palms on her pants. "I'm really nervous. Are you?"

I shrugged. "I'd rather be playing baseball."

"You're kidding. What school do you go to?"

"Truman."

"What grade?"

"Sixth. How about you?"

"I'm a freshman at West." She grinned. "This is so exciting!"

I nodded, even though I didn't think this was at all exciting.

"Okay, ladies," Ms. Landers said. "I think everyone is here, so we'll get started."

She picked up her notebook and sat in the last vacant chair in the circle.

"I'm Ms. Landers, the fashion show director and coordinator. Next to me is Samantha Pauling, my assistant. We have fourteen models here, ages twelve to eighteen. I'm very happy about the group this year, and I think we'll have a great show. You'll each be modeling four outfits. I've chosen four songs, and you'll come down the runway alone, in pairs, or in groups wearing your outfit for each song. I have the whole show choreographed, and we'll learn it at tomorrow's rehearsal."

Lisa raised her hand.

"Yes, Lisa?"

"It's choreographed? Are we going to dance?"

"We're going to move to the music and learn our cues to enter by listening to the songs."

"Oh. Well, I asked because I've taken dance lessons since I was five."

"That should be helpful," Ms. Landers said. "But not necessary."

Ms. Landers turned over a couple of pages in her notebook. "First, I'm going to give each of you your store assignments and a list of the clothes you'll be modeling during the show. Eight of the mall stores have clothes to be shown. You'll each wear something from half the stores. It'll be your responsibility, in the next week, to make an appointment for fittings."

An excited murmur ran around the circle. "That'll be so much fun!" Abby whispered.

Yuck. What a way to spend valuable baseball-playing hours.

"Samantha, will you pass out the assignments to everyone, please?" Ms. Landers asked. Samantha walked around the circle and handed out sheets of paper to each girl.

I was assigned to wear clothes from Pearson's (junior clothes), McCloud's (sporting goods and apparel), Claussen's (a ritzy store I'd never been in) and The Trap (a place that sells mostly jeans and stuff to go with them).

I glanced down the list of clothes I was supposed to model.

1. *Jeans, polo shirt, socks, cross-training shoes*
2. *Denim skirt, blouse, pumps*
3. *Swimsuit*
4. *Column dress*

I gawked at number three. A *swimsuit*? Panic gripped at my chest. I couldn't wear a swimsuit! I glanced around at the other girls in the circle. Any one of them could model a swimsuit better than I could!

I looked at Lisa. Maybe she would trade with me. I was sure she'd *love* to wear a swimsuit.

"Are there any questions?" Ms. Landers asked.

Yes! Do I have to wear a swimsuit? Could I trade with Lisa St. George, who would love to show off her chest, which is practically the size of Cincinnati?

Of course, I didn't ask.

"What are you wearing?" Abby whispered. I showed her my sheet. "A swimsuit?" Her eyes got big, and she looked over at my chest. "Wow."

I felt my cheeks heat up.

Cripes, I thought. *Everyone's going to be looking at me and laughing. Why would Ms. Landers have me wear a swimsuit? Didn't she notice what my body looks like?*

Then I realized it. It was a mistake! It had to be. I'd just point it out to her, and she'd assign the swimsuit to Lisa or some other girl who had a big shelf in front.

I relaxed and felt better.

"Ms. Landers?" said one of the oldest girls.

"Yes, Candy?"

"Who will choose the Supermodel?"

"There will be three judges," Ms. Landers said. "They'll be announced later." She smiled. "Okay, let's move over to the stage area."

I looked around. There wasn't a stage.

Ms. Landers stood and pointed to the other side of the room, where tapes stretched across the floor. "I've outlined the dimensions of the mall stage. This is where we'll rehearse. It won't be hard to transfer to the stage upstairs on the day of the show."

My stomach tightened. On the day of the

show, would I be so scared, I'd throw up? Or get a bad case of the hiccups?

Of course, I didn't really plan to stay in this fashion show, anyway, so what was I worried about?

"As you can see," Ms. Landers said, "the stage is in a T shape. You'll enter at one edge of the top of the T, walk to the corner, pause, and go to the bottom of the T. Then you'll pose a few seconds and wait for the other girls to get there. We'll have poses or movement together, then you'll return the way you came in.

"I'm going to play each of the four songs for you," she continued. "Sit on the floor and close your eyes. Imagine how you're going to move. Each song sets a different mood and requires a different kind of movement."

We sat on the floor and leaned against the wall. She played all four songs, which I'd heard on the radio. She was right; they were all different. I figured it wouldn't be too hard to walk to their rhythms.

"Would someone like to demonstrate how she'd like to move to the first song?" Ms. Landers asked.

Lisa's hand shot up. "Lisa, go ahead." Ms.

Landers looked at her notebook. "You'll start at stage right." She pointed. "Stage directions are as you face the audience."

"I knew that," Lisa said, smiling smugly.

Ms. Landers turned on the music, and Lisa began an amazing dance. She jumped, she whirled, and she danced, smiling and throwing her hair from side to side. Ms. Landers said, "Uh, Lisa—" and faded the volume down to nothing. Lisa jumped once more for good measure, then slid into a split and threw her arms up as if she had just finished leading a cheer.

"Lisa, that's very . . . interesting," Ms. Landers said. "But I should remind you that we're not dancing here, we're *moving* to music. We're not here to show ourselves off. The focus will be on the clothes and how we present the fashions."

Ms. Landers looked around. "Does anyone have an idea about what I mean?"

Lisa got up, red-faced, and returned to her spot next to the wall.

"I think I do." It was the Living Barbie Doll that I'd seen in Ms. Landers' office before my interview.

"Karen, give it a try. You'll be entering from stage left."

Karen was great. She walked onstage, looking happy, and smiled with those blindingly white teeth. She paused at the corner, looked around—still smiling—and continued to the bottom of the T. She turned around with a flourish to the music, then returned.

"Very good," Ms. Landers said. "I'd suggest a little less swing of the arms, though." She looked around at all of us. "Let's all try it together."

So we did, as if we were in a parade. "I'm going to see the Cubbies, I'm going to see the Cubbies," I whispered to myself over and over. That is, I'd see the Cubbies *if* I decided to be in the fashion show. And I probably wouldn't.

Mary Ann was right, though. Thinking about seeing a Cubs game helped me block out most of my feelings of embarrassment at doing something this silly.

We practiced moving to all four songs while Ms. Landers watched and made notes. Afterward, she said, "Okay, let's go back to the chairs, and I'll give you my critique."

When we were all seated, she talked to each of us in the circle.

"Mary, smile more. You look worried."

"Lisa, I like your enthusiasm. But remember, we want the focus on the fashions. No one girl should stand out from the others."

"Karen, your arm swing is just about perfect now."

"Lizard, nice job, but loosen up a little more. And you'll need to get a bra tomorrow or the next day at the latest."

She moved on, talking to each girl, but I didn't hear a word of it.

She'd said I needed a bra—in front of *everybody*!

I stared at the floor, my face burning fiercely. My vision blurred and my head buzzed. She might as well have announced it to the whole mall over the public address system:

"Lizard Flanagan, please come to the mall office and get yourself a bra as soon as possible!"

When she stopped talking, I hurried out as fast as I could. I didn't want to see anyone. I didn't even think of asking Ms. Landers about the mistake with the swimsuit.

I just wanted to get out of there.

This was the dumbest thing I'd ever done in my life. How did I let myself get sucked into this horrible fashion show?

It's not too late, I told myself. *I can still get out of it.*

But how?

CHAPTER EIGHT

"**H**OW'D IT GO?**" Mary Ann stood on the front porch, peering through the screen. We'd just finished supper.

"Horrible." I went out on the porch and gave her a nudge. "Let's go in the backyard. I don't want anybody to hear this."

We walked around back and through the gate. My dog, Bob, was barking at a squirrel or something, but he bounded over to us. I dragged Mary Ann to the maple tree, away from the open windows.

"So what happened?" Mary Ann asked, scratching Bob's neck while he slobbered on her.

"At the end of the practice, Ms. Landers gave us comments. She said—in front of everybody—that I should get a bra!"

Mary Ann looked horrified. "Lisa heard?"

"*Everybody* heard! I can't go back. It's too embarrassing."

"Especially with Lisa there," Mary Ann said.

A stick fell on my head, and I brushed it off.

"I'm not going back."

"But don't you want to go to Chicago?" Mary Ann said. "You've come so far."

"Besides, I'll probably start hiccuping during the show, anyway."

"You won't hiccup."

"Right," I said. "Just like in fourth grade."

"I'll go to the mall with you after school tomorrow," Mary Ann said. "We'll get you a bra."

I thought about that. "Well, I suppose I should get one."

"It's time."

"It is?"

"Yes. You should start wearing a bra."

A high, screechy voice came from overhead. "Yeah, Lizard, you should start wearing a bra!"

Horrified, I looked up into the tree. Sam was sitting up in the branches, laughing!

"You *jerk*!" I yelled. "You creep, you eaves-dropper! Come down here; I'll knock your head off!"

"Come on, Lizard." Mary Ann grabbed my arm, but I shook her off furiously.

"Come down here, Sam!"

"Go get your bra, Lizard!" he screeched. "It's time!"

"I'm going to kill him," I said. I grabbed hold of a lower branch and started to pull myself into the tree. Mary Ann hauled me back down.

"Come on, Lizard," she said. "Let's go for a walk."

"I don't want to walk. I want to seriously injure my brother."

"Lizard!" Mary Ann kept a firm grip on me. I knew she wouldn't give up and let me climb into the tree.

"Let's get out of here," I said, and I stalked out the gate.

"Go get that bra, Lizard!" the rat called after me, loud enough so the whole neighbor-hood could hear.

"I'm going to kill him."

"Let's go to the mall tomorrow," Mary Ann

repeated. "We'll get you a bra."

"I'll have to wait for just the right moment, when he isn't expecting it."

"The clerk who waited on me last summer was very nice."

"Maybe I can set up a booby trap in his room."

"Lizard?"

"What?"

"Let's go to the mall tomorrow and get you a bra."

"You really think I need one?"

"Yes."

"Okay. But I'm not going back to those rehearsals. And the next time I get Sam alone—"

"Tomorrow after school," she said.

"Whatever."

I saw Ginger at our locker the next morning. Five seconds, I thought, and she'll say it. Four, three—Ginger turned and saw me—two, one . . .

"I heard what Ms. Landers said to you in front of the whole world!" Ginger said.

Right on cue. But I was ready for her. Mary

Ann and I had talked about how I'd handle it.

I shrugged. "Yeah," I said, as casual as you please. I pulled out my language arts notebook.

"You're so calm!" Ginger said. "I really admire you. I would've been humiliated." She lowered her voice. "So are you going to get a . . . you know?"

"A bra?" I looked at Ginger squarely in the eyes. "Yes, I am." I closed the locker. "See you, Ginger. Gotta go to my first class."

"Okay." Her voice came out soft. I think she was disappointed that we weren't going to have a big talk about the bra thing.

I walked away, and that was that.

Nothing disastrous happened that morning, but I figured the "Lizard needs a bra" story had been broadcast to all the girls by Lisa and my bigmouth locker partner. I was glad I'd worn a big, floppy shirt that day. If anybody looked, they wouldn't see anything.

I had the feeling that the guys hadn't heard it. At least my rotten brother had the decency to keep his mouth shut.

At lunch Ed Mechtensteimer told us how he'd seen Matthew Dunn writing on the concrete wall outside the school building.

"Boy, you should've seen Wildwoman go after him!" Mechtensteimer said. "I bet Dunn gets a hundred detentions for that."

"Oh, yeah, right," Stinky scoffed. "A hundred!"

"I'd expel him," I said. "Matthew Dunn is such a lowlife. Remember when he threw that firecracker onto the field during our metro game last year, Zach?"

"Hunh?"

"He's daydreaming," Stinky said. "I bet he's thinking about biting Cassandra March's neck."

"I would be," Ed said. "Hey, when are you doing your scene?"

Zach swallowed. "In two weeks."

"Yeah, after school," Stinky said. "And anyone can come. We'll be there, Walters, right in the front row, watching every move!"

"Are ya having fun practicing?" Ed asked, his eyes bugging out at the thought of taking a bite out of Cassandra March.

Zach shrugged. "It's okay."

Stinky, sitting next to him, gave him a shove. "I bet it's more than okay, Walters!" he said. Zach shoved him back.

Stinky grinned at Ed. "Have you noticed that Cassandra's been wearing lots of perfume lately?"

"You must be getting pretty close yourself, Stinky, to notice that," I said.

"I don't have to," he said. "She walks into a room, and you can smell it all over. But yesterday I wanted to check it out, so when she was sharpening her pencil, I leaned over and sniffed. And you know what?"

"What?" Ed was all ears.

"That's right where she puts the perfume," Stinky said, his voice ringing with authority. "On her *neck*."

"She's doing it for Zach," Ed said. "She wants to smell good when he bites her neck every day."

"She is not," Zach said. But he didn't say it very strongly. Maybe he thought she was wearing perfume for him too.

Was she? I didn't know Cassandra very well. She was in the black group, but I'd seen her in the halls plenty of times. She's hard to miss, because she's very pretty. And I hated to admit it, but she seemed nice. At least, that's what everyone said.

I'd reconsider how I felt about her, though,

if she was dousing herself with perfume for Zach.

Was Zach spaced out because of Cassandra? He had been acting kind of strange lately. I tried to remember when he had started getting weird and distracted. It *was* about the time he started practicing the *Dracula* scene.

I watched Zach for the rest of lunch, my heart aching. I hoped he wasn't in love with Cassandra. Aside from being my boyfriend, he was one of the best friends I'd ever had, and I didn't want to lose him.

"There she is," Mary Ann whispered. She nodded to the clerk behind the lingerie counter at Bregmann's Department Store. "She helped me and my mom find my size last summer."

"Let's just find your size and try it and get the heck out of here," I said.

"Okay, it was on the rack over there, thirty-two B. Come on."

Mary Ann walked over to the display, and I tiptoed behind her, hoping we wouldn't attract the clerk's attention. This was embarrassing enough without having to talk to a stranger about it.

Mary Ann pulled a bra off the rack and held it up. "Here's one."

"Mary Ann, quit waving it around, okay?" I murmured out the side of my mouth.

A movement at my right startled me.

"Hi, Lizard," said Lisa, who had mysteriously materialized next to me. Had she followed us from school? She must've known where we'd be going.

Mary Ann looked horrified and whipped the bra she was holding behind her back.

Lisa was the last person on earth I wanted to see. I stared at her and said pointedly, "Hi, Lisa. What are *you* doing here?"

Lisa smiled smugly. "The same thing you're doing." She looked around. "I must be in the wrong section. I was looking for the thirty-four C sizes. These are much too small."

For the second time in two days, my face fired up. I had to restrain myself from smacking that smile off her face. She turned and oozed away, swinging her hips from side to side.

"Wouldn't it be great if she fell flat on

her face in the fashion show?" I suggested. "Maybe I could trip her."

"Come on," Mary Ann said. "Let's go back so you can try this on. I'll wait outside."

I walked back to the dressing room. Inside the swinging doors, I pulled off my shirt and took the bra off the hanger.

"How do you get this thing on?" I asked Mary Ann in a low voice.

"The way you put on the top of a two-piece swimsuit."

"When have you ever seen me in a two-piecer?" I said.

"Oh, yeah. Hook it in the front and slide it to the back."

That worked pretty well. "Come on in," I said.

Mary Ann slipped into the dressing room. She frowned, looking at me critically. "I think it's too big. It puckers out a little. That'll get smashed under a T-shirt, and you'll be able to see it. It should look smooth. I'll get you a thirty-two A."

"Thirty-two A?"

"The number is the measurement around your rib cage. The letter is the cup size. You need a smaller cup."

Good grief. A thirty-two A. What was Lisa's? Thirty-four C?

"Would you get it, Mary Ann?" I asked. "But if you see Lisa anywhere in the store, *don't* pick it up."

"Gotcha."

Mary Ann left. I looked at myself in the mirror. It was weird seeing myself in a bra. It felt weird, too, with all the straps, sort of like those straitjackets they put on crazy people in the movies.

Mary Ann came back. "Lisa must've left." She poked the bra in between the doors.

"Good." I took off the first bra and put on the smaller one. It was tight on the shoulders, so Mary Ann showed me how to lengthen the straps. It felt better, and the cups were smooth. Mary Ann agreed that it was a better fit.

"Let's get two for now," she said.

"Okay." Mom had given me the money when I told her why I needed it. "Will you get the other one? But look out for Lisa."

"Okay."

I met Mary Ann at the cash register.

"I'll go find the clerk," Mary Ann said. She disappeared behind a rack of nightgowns.

Suddenly Lisa appeared out of nowhere again. I clutched the bras close so she couldn't see their size.

I scowled at her. "What are you doing, following me?"

"Why would I do that?" she said, in an innocent voice.

"I sure wouldn't know."

I stood there, trying to think of a plan. How could I buy these bras without Lisa's getting a look at them? Just then, Mary Ann and the clerk came weaving around the racks of lingerie.

I caught Mary Ann's eye and nodded slightly at Lisa. Mary Ann's mouth opened, then closed.

She walked directly over to Lisa and tapped her on the shoulder. "Lisa, did you enjoy the first practice for the fashion show?"

Good old Mary Ann. She was trying to distract Lisa.

I planted myself between Lisa and the bras.

"It was okay," Lisa said.

The clerk picked up the bras and scanned the tags. "Was the thirty-two A a good fit?" she asked, her voice booming through the store as if she'd yelled into a microphone.

Lisa snorted.

Mary Ann's face went white, and I came close to lunging over the counter to strangle that clerk. I wished I could vaporize into the floor, but I came to my senses and mumbled, "It's very snug, but it'll have to do. We took the straps out as far as they'd go."

I slapped the money on the counter, and the woman finished ringing up the sale.

I stalked past Lisa. She waved and called out, "I'll see you at practice tonight, Lizard."

When Mary Ann and I were outside the mall, I said, "This isn't worth it."

"It's not worth sitting at Wrigley Field and seeing the great Mark Grace and Sammy Sosa in person?"

I sighed heavily. "I want to go to the game, but this is terrible. That was even worse than Ms. Landers telling me in front of everybody that I need a bra! My bra size will be broadcast all over school before our first class tomorrow morning."

"There's no relationship between bra size and brainpower or talent," Mary Ann said.

"No kidding," I agreed. "Look at Lisa."

"Just keep concentrating on why you're

doing this," Mary Ann told me.

"I'm going to see the Cubbies, I'm going to see the Cubbies."

"That's right."

"I'm going to punch Lisa's lights out, I'm going to punch Lisa's lights out."

Mary Ann laughed. "I'll help you. She's such a wimp, that'll be easy."

"I think I'll daydream about that for a while," I said. "That makes me feel better than anything right now."

"Good, then do it."

On the way home, I imagined cutting off all of Lisa's hair while she slept, dousing her with superglue and rolling her around on piles of dryer lint.

When I got home, I felt a lot better.

CHAPTER NINE

MS. LANDERS DIDN'T SAY anything at rehearsal that night about my wearing a bra. I was glad about that, but I hoped she noticed I was wearing one.

I'd decided that after the rehearsal, I'd point out the mistake she'd made, assigning me to model the swimsuit. I thought we should get that cleared up right away.

She taught us the choreography for the four songs. It wasn't hard. Mostly, it was learning where our entrances and exits were in the music, when to do turns, when to raise our arms together, and when to pose. Stuff like that.

I felt pretty dumb doing it, but I kept imagining myself sitting between Zach and Mary Ann at Wrigley Field. That picture in my mind helped me to smile when I was supposed to.

We practiced the songs over and over till I was sick of them. Ms. Landers gave us critiques at the end of each song. I was waiting for her to say something embarrassing to me, but all she said was, "Lizard, you were two beats slow in coming out on the first song," and "Remember to smile a lot."

At the end of the rehearsal, I stood around so I could talk to Ms. Landers about the swimsuit without anyone else listening. I didn't mind if her assistant, Samantha, heard the conversation. She seemed nice. But I didn't want any of the other girls to hear. Especially Lisa.

Someone came up behind me, pulled out my bra strap and let it smack against me, stinging my back.

"I see you're wearing your little bra—"

I whirled around and shoved Lisa so hard she fell backward on her butt.

"Owwww!" she yelled as she hit the floor.

"Don't ever do that again, Lisa St. George!" I shouted.

"What's going on here?" Ms. Landers strode over from her table. Samantha followed close behind. I guess they weren't used to their models getting into fights.

"Lizard shoved me over backward!" Lisa wailed, wrapping one hand around her wrist.

Ms. Landers looked horrified. "Why did you do it, Lizard?"

"Lisa's been making fun— Oh, never mind. She had it coming." I glared at Lisa. "Get out of my face."

"Lisa," Ms. Landers said firmly, "if you're hassling Lizard, stop it right now! And Lizard, I don't want to see you shove anyone again. Either one of you—or both—will be out of the show if I see any more of this kind of behavior."

"She pushed me!" Lisa whined.

"Not one more word!"

Ms. Landers, at that moment, looked an awful lot like my mom when she's mad.

I turned and stalked out of the store.

I hadn't talked to Ms. Landers about her mistake, but I could do that later. I had to get out of there fast, before I punched in Lisa's perfect, snotty little nose.

Ginger was waiting for me at our locker in the morning.

"I don't want to talk about it," I said. "Lisa had it coming."

"Oh, I wasn't going to say anything about you shoving Lisa on the floor," Ginger said, twisting a strand of hair between two fingers. "I just thought that, as your friend, I should tell you about Zach and Cassandra."

My ears pricked up, but I didn't say anything. I threw my homework books into the locker.

"You know they're doing that scene from *Dracula*, don't you?"

"Yeah." I pulled out a notebook and slammed the locker closed.

"And you know Zach has to bite Cassandra's neck, don't you?"

"So?" I started walking away.

"Well, Lizard, I think you should know . . ." She scurried alongside me to keep up. "They're falling in love."

I stopped in the middle of the hall. "That's a crock."

Ginger sighed. "I know, the jilted one is always the last to know. But it's true. Just ask anybody." She put her hand on my arm sympathetically, but I shook it off. "I'm only telling you as your true friend. I know how totally devastated you must be. Talk about major ruin-your-life news! Call me anytime you want to talk about it."

What I wanted to say was "Buzz off," and I almost did. But she had real sympathy in her eyes, so I couldn't say anything mean. I wasn't in the mood to say something nice, though, so I walked away.

"Just remember, I'm on your side, Lizard!" she called after me.

I rounded a corner and spotted Cassandra drinking at the water fountain. I walked over and waited behind her. She leaned over, sipping water and holding her hair to one side so it wouldn't get wet.

Her neck was right there in front of me. The neck that Zach was biting every day at his rehearsals.

I had to admit, it was a nice neck. Slender and long, not like a giraffe's, but graceful and curved like a dancer's. I was sure it was the kind of neck a boy would like to bite.

She straightened up and wiped a drop of water from her mouth.

"Oh, hi, Lizard," she said.

So she knew who I was. I'm sure she'd heard that I was Zach's girlfriend.

"Hi."

She smelled of perfume, just as Stinky had said.

I really wanted to dislike Cassandra for wearing that perfume. Zach was my best friend and my boyfriend, and I had a right to hate her for trying to steal him away from me. I waited for her to say something that would really make me mad. But she didn't say anything; she just smiled.

"How's *Dracula* going?" I asked finally. Would she say something about Zach?

"Fine." She looked down at the floor a second. "It's embarrassing, though. Everybody's teasing me about the neck bite."

"I know," I said. I watched her face carefully. Did she really like the teasing? Was she just trying to keep on my good side so I wouldn't get mad? "Zach's getting teased a lot too."

"I wish they would stop," Cassandra said. "It's dumb."

"Yeah."

I tried so hard to hate her, but how could I? She seemed so nice. Anybody would like her. I thought she meant it when she said she wished everyone would stop teasing her and Zach.

"Oooh, there they are," Stinky said. He stood next to Ed Mechtensteimer in the middle of the hall. Ed looked awkward and embarrassed, but Stinky was grinning. "Rivals for Zach's affections. Are they going to punch it out?"

"Shut up, Stinky," I said.

"Don't hit her, Lizard," he said. "She might have a great right hook. Then you'd be flattened right here in the hallway, and you know what Wildwoman would do about that! You'd get detentions, lots of them! You might even get expelled."

"Come on, Cassandra," I said. "Let's get away from these jerks."

She smiled at me, looking relieved. "Yeah, let's go."

"Wow, did you see that?" Stinky said behind us. "They're acting like friends!"

We walked down the hall. "What's your first class?" I asked her.

"Language arts."

"Oh, yeah. Mrs. Brown. How do you like her?"

"She's nice." Cassandra stopped. "Hey, Lizard?"

"Yeah?"

"I know that Zach is your boyfriend," she said. "I want you to know that I'm not trying to take him away from you or anything. I've heard what the kids are saying."

"Well . . . thanks, Cassandra."

"Sure."

"Hey," I said, "you don't play baseball, do you?"

"No. I'm the last person chosen for *any* kind of team in P.E."

I grinned. "Great!" I forced the smile off my face. "I mean, that's too bad. I was just wondering. See you."

"See you."

I felt like jumping up and down and whooping, but of course I didn't. Cassandra really *was* a nice person. It was great news that she wasn't trying to steal Zach away from me, and that she wanted me to know—

I stopped suddenly just outside Squirrely Pearly's class. A thought came to me then like a thunderbolt.

What if Zach was falling in love with *her*? What if she wanted me to know that she wasn't *trying* to steal Zach away from me, but he wanted to be her boyfriend anyway?

That rotten feeling came back to my

stomach. I decided to talk to Zach again and see how he reacted when I asked him about Cassandra. After school would be a good time.

I'd watch his face, and then I'd know for sure.

"Tell them what your mom told you," Ginger said.

P.E. class was about to begin, and most of the girls were sitting around Lisa's feet while she sat on the lowest level of the bleachers. They'd been treating her like royalty since she'd been named as one of the models in the Spring Pines fashion show. They were sure she'd be chosen Supermodel and they wanted to be on her good side when it launched her into a career in high fashion modeling.

Ginger led the fawning fest. "Tell them," she urged Lisa. "Your mom is *so* understanding."

Lisa smiled. "Well, my mother has excused me from all chores until the fashion show is over. I don't have to wash dishes or rake leaves or pull out the tomato plants or wash the car or anything."

The girls oohed.

"Gee, Lisa, I wish I could get out of chores,"

Tiffany said. "Your mother's fantastic."

"Well, she understands how important it is for me to protect my hands," Lisa sniffed. "If a talent scout is in the audience, and I get into professional modeling after this, I might be used as a hand model sometime."

"What's a hand model?" Heather asked.

"If you see a closeup of a hand doing something on TV or in a magazine, the person that the hand belongs to is a hand model. People who are hand models don't do physical labor. They can't afford to have dishpan hands or to break nails or get dirt or stains on their skin."

"Oh, but no one would want to show just your hands, Lisa!" gushed Ginger. "Your face is so beautiful."

"Well, you never know what kind of morons might be doing the commercial," Lisa said.

Mrs. Puff walked in, her clipboard under her arm.

"Just a minute," Lisa said. "I have to talk to Mrs. Puff."

She jumped up from her seat and approached the teacher, flipping her long hair over her shoulder.

"Mrs. Puff," Lisa said, "I don't know if you know this, but I'm modeling in the Spring Pines fashion show."

"Oh, yes. I heard about that." Mrs. Puff started checking off names on her roll sheet. "Amanda Adams? Is she here?"

"She's at the orthodontist getting braces," Sara Pulliam chirped.

"Anyway," Lisa said, "my mother and I think I should be excused from gym until the show is over."

Mrs. Puff stopped and turned to Lisa, surprised. "Whatever for?"

"Well, what if I get hit in the face with a ball and get disfigured?" Lisa said. "It could ruin my career in high fashion modeling."

A laugh escaped my mouth before I could stop it. Lisa glared at me, then turned back to Mrs. Puff.

"I don't think that's likely," Mrs. Puff said. "You don't have a letter from your mother, do you?"

"Well, no, but—"

"Then I suggest you join the other girls on the floor while I call the roll."

"But, Mrs. Puff, I have to think of my future."

"Sit down, Lisa."

"My future—"

"Your future is going to be in the principal's office if you don't drop it."

Lisa huffed loudly, but walked back and sat down, defeated. Ginger patted her arm and whispered to her, "Don't worry. If you get disfigured, you could sue the pants off the school district."

Lisa's face brightened, then her smile faded when she realized that meant she'd have to have her looks ruined.

The kids swarmed out of the building like bees out of a hive. I stood next to the flagpole, looking for Zach. I'd told Mary Ann that I'd asked him to ride home with me today. She knew why. She'd been hearing the rumors, too.

He came loping out the door in the middle of a crowd. He waved at me.

"Hi," I said.

He walked past me, and I followed him to the bike rack. We unlocked our bikes and stuffed the chains in our backpacks. Then we headed into the street.

I rode behind him for several blocks in

the heavy traffic. But when we turned off the busiest street, I rode up next to him.

"Want to stop at Whetstone's and get some taffy to eat at the ravine?" I asked him.

"Okay."

We stopped at Whetstone's, then veered off the street after half a block and left our bikes at the rim of the shallow ravine. We ran down the side and stopped next to the stream that flows across the bottom.

This is a special place to me. Whenever I want to have a talk about something important with Zach or Mary Ann, I like to come here with them. Sometimes, I take off my shoes and socks and cool my toes in the water while we talk.

Today, though, we tossed our book bags on the leafy bank and sat together on the fallen log next to the water.

My stomach fluttered nervously. I tried to be ready for whatever Zach would say. Maybe he would tell me that he liked Cassandra better than he liked me. Maybe this would be a horrible conversation, and we'd break up.

I'd thought a lot about how I'd start off the conversation, so I jumped right in.

"How'd your *Dracula* rehearsal go today?" I asked him. I handed him his taffy and unwrapped my piece, even though I didn't feel like eating it.

He took the taffy and sighed heavily. "Fine."

That didn't get me anywhere, so I tried again. "Is it hard to learn all your lines?"

"I don't have any lines." He stared at the taffy in his hand, then stuck it in his back pants pocket. He leaned his elbows on his knees and looked into the water that gurgled along the stream bed.

Was he trying to think of a way to tell me he wanted to break up?

"Well," I said, my heart hammering away in my chest, "it sure must be more fun than doing dumb old language arts stuff."

"Yeah."

Zach was never this quiet! If he had something to tell me about Cassandra, why didn't he just say it? I decided the only way to find out once and for all was to ask. I pulled the wrapper up and folded it over the candy and was surprised that my hands were shaking a little.

"Zach? I've been hearing things about you and Cassandra."

"What things?" He was still staring at the water.

"That you . . . that you . . . really like her."

"She's real nice."

"I know. I think so too." I thought a moment. Would he tell me he was in love with Cassandra if I asked? I braced myself. "I mean, all the guys are saying that you want to be her boyfriend."

Zach didn't even blink; he just stared. I couldn't tell if he even heard what I said.

"Zach?"

"Hunh?"

"Do you really like Cassandra?"

"Sure." He sat up and looked at me, but I had the strange feeling he wasn't really seeing me. "Did I ever tell you about what happened to my uncle when he was a kid?"

"Your uncle?" I was surprised that he'd changed the subject so suddenly. "Which one?"

"Uncle Elmer."

"I haven't heard of him." Was Zach going to tell me something serious, or was this one of his crazy stories?

"When Uncle Elmer was a kid, he took a shortcut home from school one day. He had to walk through a thick forest. It was dark and cool, and hardly any light penetrated the umbrella of leaves overhead. But he knew if he kept walking, he'd come out on the other side, just a block from his house.

"After an hour of walking, though, he realized he was lost. Maybe he'd been walking in circles. This was supposed to be a shortcut, and walking *around* the forest only took twenty-three minutes."

"Some shortcut," I said.

"Elmer came upon an old house. It looked a little like my house, with a big front porch. But it was very run-down."

"Who lived there?"

"The grown-up granddaughter of the witch in the Hansel and Gretel story."

I grinned. It was good to hear one of his wild stories after so much weird silence.

"She inherited nasty genes from her grandmother. She captured Uncle Elmer and made him a prisoner under the porch. It was dark and cold under there, and rats and snakes came in at night and nibbled on his toes. He screamed and yelled, but he was so deep in the forest, no one could hear. He nearly went crazy. The only food he had was potato chips and Coke, which the witch fed him once a day through the openings in the trellis."

"At least it wasn't lentil and spinach surprise," I said, thinking of one of my mom's favorite dishes. "Did he finally get away?"

"The witch had termites that ate through the wooden trellis, and he escaped. But my uncle was changed forever after his imprisonment under the porch. He can't stand small spaces. He's forty-three now, but he won't ride in elevators, even though he lives in an apartment on the fourteenth floor. He turned into the skinniest man alive because he runs up and down the stairs all the time. You can look him up in the *Guinness Book of World Records*."

"Your relatives sure have interesting experiences," I said, grinning. While it was good to hear one of his stories, this was different from the others. Usually his stories have happy endings. The poor, skinny uncle who wouldn't ride elevators sure didn't live happily ever after.

I wondered if Zach wanted to tell me that our story wasn't going to have a happy ending either.

"Tell me more about your *Dracula* scene."

He stood up. "I'm going home."

What in the world was wrong with Zach? I'd never seen him acting so weird.

It had to be Cassandra. He must be falling in love with her, just like Ginger said, and he didn't have the heart to tell me. I had a deep ache in the middle of my chest.

I climbed the side of the ravine behind him, and we rode our bikes down the street. When we got to his house he turned in without even saying good-bye.

CHAPTER TEN

"**G**IRLS," **MS. LANDERS** called out at rehearsal that evening. "Have you all scheduled fittings for the clothes you're going to model?"

Everyone nodded except me. I hadn't called any of the stores because I hadn't talked to Ms. Landers yet about the swimsuit. I figured if that was wrong, maybe my whole list was wrong. Ms. Landers's gaze stopped on me.

"Lizard, have you contacted the stores on your list?"

"No, but I will. Can I talk to you after the rehearsal?"

"Sure."

We practiced the four songs, and Ms. Landers gave us her critique. She told me I should swing my hips a little more in the up-tempo song. "That should loosen you up just a bit," she said.

Good grief. I wasn't even sure my hips *could* swing. They'd never swung before, as far as I knew.

After she'd finished her comments, Ms. Landers gestured to seven mirrors with lights around them set up on some long tables.

"Tonight I'm going to talk to you all about makeup," she said. "Come and gather round the first makeup mirror."

We clustered around a chair where Samantha sat, facing the mirror.

"In fashion modeling, simple is better," Ms. Landers said. "I'd like you all to wear some foundation."

"We'll pair up and choose the right shade. Test it on your wrist." She held up a bottle of tannish stuff.

"Use your fingers to apply it," Ms. Landers said. "They're better at smoothing it into the nooks and crannies around your eyes and nose. Your fingers also warm it and make it easier to spread. Start at the center of your face, then blend it outward."

She smoothed it over Samantha's face, till her skin looked smooth and pale, as if she were wearing a tight mask.

"Next, the eyes. We want shadow with a soft color. Use the lightest shade over your lid, and apply a darker shade along your crease line and the outer corner." She demonstrated. "Then blend."

I was starting to get bored, but the other girls were leaning in to see every stroke Ms. Landers made with the brush. I just wanted to get the swimsuit thing cleared up with Ms. Landers and go home and sort my baseball cards.

Ms. Landers continued to drone on about makeup, then we had to pair up and practice putting it on. I ended up with Abby Bowen, the freshman with the crayon eyebrows I'd met on the first night of rehearsal. Since I hadn't listened very well, I made a few mistakes. Abby asked me to hand her the mascara, and I couldn't remember what it was. I figured it was either the long thin thing, or the round flat deal, but I didn't know which. I shrugged and handed her the round flat deal.

"No, the mascara," she said.

"Oh, I didn't hear what you said."

The rest of the makeup practice went

okay, even though it was awfully boring.

After the rehearsal was over, I waited until everyone was gone so I could talk to Ms. Landers in private.

"Yes, Lizard, you wanted to see me?" she said, shuffling through some papers at the table.

"Yes," I said. "I think you may have made a mistake." I handed her my sheet with the clothes assignments. She scanned the paper and looked up.

"A mistake?"

"Number three. The swimsuit."

"That's not a mistake, Lizard." She handed it back.

"It's not?"

"It's a competition swimsuit. A lot of young girls in this area are competing with the Swimming Association. You're the perfect choice to model it because of your athletic build."

"But—but—" How could I tell her? "I don't have . . . I mean, well, Ms. Landers, in case you haven't noticed, I'm—well, I'm pretty thin all over."

Ms. Landers smiled. "You have a fine body, Lizard. You're athletic and strong. That's why

I chose you to model the swimsuit. You're as strong as the girls who're going to swimming competitions. They'll identify with you."

"Wouldn't you like to pick someone like Lisa? I'm sure she'd love to model the swimsuit."

Ms. Landers laughed. "I'm sure she would. But I want you to model it. You're the best choice, believe me."

"But—" How could I tell her that I'd feel practically naked up there? And skinnier than a rail?

"Lizard," Ms. Landers said, "you should be so proud of yourself! You're not only a lovely girl, you're healthy and strong. That's what I want to project here. I want a lean, strong—and pretty—image. That's you. You're the perfect choice."

It was flattering to hear an adult who wasn't in my family describe me that way. And she looked so sure she was right, I had the feeling I could stand there for the next three days, and I wouldn't change her mind.

"Okay." But I still didn't want to wear the swimsuit in the fashion show. I'd lost my argument, and I didn't know what else to say.

"You'll be very proud of yourself, Lizard,"

Ms. Landers said. "Wait and see."

Mom picked me up outside the mall. I didn't talk all the way home. When we pulled into the driveway, she asked me if I was okay. "Yes," I said, "everything's fine."

But it wasn't fine. It was all mixed up. My boyfriend had fallen in love with a girl because of her perfumed neck, and I was going to be horribly embarrassed by being nearly naked in front of a whole audience full of people.

Up until now, I'd been fairly good at getting myself out of scrapes. But this time was different.

If Zach was falling in love with Cassandra, I figured that even though it hurt a lot, I'd have to accept it. We could still be friends. But the fashion show was something I could do something about! There was no law that said I had to be in it, or that I had to wear a swimsuit.

I either had to think of a solution or get out of the show. And I'd better do it fast! The fashion show was only ten days away.

CHAPTER ELEVEN

THE NEXT DAY AFTER SCHOOL, I was getting my homework books out of my locker when I heard Ginger say, "Hey, Sammy! You want to come to the mall with Lisa and Heather and me?"

"I've got football practice," he said, grinning like an idiot at her. He shoved one hand into a back pocket and shifted his weight onto one foot, then the other.

"Maybe we'll stop by your practice for a while," she said. She twisted from side to side and blushed, grinning even more idiotically than he did, which I didn't think was possible.

With them both shifting and squirming in front of each other, they looked like two people doing a bizarre dance, only there wasn't any music.

"We're looking pretty good, Coach says," Sam bragged.

"You guys look pretty good, anyway!" Ginger blurted out, then shrieked, turned a full circle and slapped her hand over her mouth as if the comment had just slipped out.

I can't believe how weird some people act with the opposite sex. I shook my head and started toward the door.

"Hey, Lizard," Sam called out. "Zach and Ed and Stinky are coming over after supper to pass the football around. You want to get Mary Ann, and we'll get up a game?"

"Sure."

Ginger laughed. "How can you practice football for two hours and then go home and play again? You must be so strong!"

"Yeah, well . . ." Sam said with a deeper voice than usual, trying to act modest. I nearly threw up.

"It's all those muscles!" Ginger said, wrapping her hands around one of his arms.

I saw Sam flex the biceps on his arm where Ginger was touching him, and a laugh escaped me before I could stop it.

"Be sure to bring all those muscles home

right after practice, Sam," I told him. "It's your night to set the table."

Sam glared at me, but I laughed again and walked away.

"You have to wear a swimsuit?" Mary Ann's eyes nearly bugged out of her head. We were sitting on my back porch waiting for the guys to come and play football. Bob was sitting at our feet, his tongue hanging out of his mouth.

"Well, I'm not going to," I said, rolling the ball around on my lap. "I have to figure out how I can get out of the fashion show."

"Isn't it too late?"

"I won't wear a swimsuit onstage and parade around in front of everyone."

"How are you going to get out of it?"

"I haven't figured it out yet." I tossed the football in the air and caught it. "Mary Ann, have you noticed how strange Zach is acting lately?" I leaned closer to her. "I think the kids at school may be right, that he's fallen in love with Cassandra."

"He seems really out of it," Mary Ann agreed. "But how do you know it's because of Cassandra?"

"What else could it be? Whenever I ask him about the *Dracula* scene, he doesn't want to talk about it. And if I ask him about Cassandra, he just says she's really nice."

"She *is* nice."

"I know. I'm afraid he wants to be her boyfriend."

"Sometimes Al Pickering is the same way," Mary Ann said.

"Really?"

"Well, most of the time he seems really glad to see me, but once in a while he doesn't act interested. I asked my sister about that, and she says she learned in her health class that it's changing hormones. She says teenagers are supposed to be moody."

"So you think Zach's just moody? That's all it is?"

"It's possible."

We didn't get to talk anymore about it because at that moment, Ed and Stinky and Zach trooped through the gate. Bob barked and bounded over to them.

"Hi, guys," I said. "Ready to play?"

"Yeah," Ed said. The guys greeted Bob with pats and scratches on his neck.

Zach smiled at me for a second, then said,

"Hi, Sam," to my brother, who was charging out the back door.

"Let's go," Sam said, clapping his hands.

We moved deeper into the backyard, away from the maple tree, with Bob following us.

"Stay," I said to Bob, pushing him into a sitting position. He wagged his tail and stood up again. "Sit," I said, and pushed him down again. "If you get in the way, I'll have to put you inside."

We chose up teams, and it was Zach, Mary Ann, and me against Sam, Ed, and Stinky. They won the toss, and Sam said they'd receive.

Zach kicked off, and the ball sailed nearly to the telephone wires before coming down into Ed's outstretched hands. Ed dodged Mary Ann. I ran for him but was blocked by Sam. Zach easily got by Stinky and rammed into Ed, tackling him and knocking him to the ground.

"Hey!" Mechtensteimer said. "This is *touch* football, Walters." He got up and gave Zach a shove.

Zach shoved back. "Consider yourself touched," he said.

Ed rubbed his elbow. It was scraped and bleeding a little. "Man, that wasn't fair."

"A tackle doesn't count," Mary Ann said.

On the next play, Mary Ann handed the ball off to Zach. I moved farther down the yard, my hands up, waiting for Zach to pass it to me. I was ready, and with Mary Ann covering me, I was in a great position to run for a touchdown.

Zach saw me and threw. It was a wild pass. The ball went sailing over the fence into the neighbor's yard.

"Zach!" I yelled. "What kind of pass was that?"

"It was the Crazy Ball-Over-the-Fence pass!" Ed hollered, grinning. Stinky laughed.

I was beginning to get ticked off at Zach. This problem he was having, raging hormones or not, was affecting his game, and that really bugged me.

"Will you get your head in the game?" I yelled at him.

He scowled and ran out the gate to get the ball. A few seconds later, he hollered, "Let's see you catch *this,* Lizard!"

I couldn't see him on the other side of the fence, but a moment later, the ball was heaved with amazing fury into the air. It flew high above the fence and arced out over the yard.

"I got it," I called out. I watched the ball sail through the air. I gauged my position under the ball so I'd be there to receive it when it came down.

I ran backward as the ball sailed in my direction, Bob barking furiously behind me. I reached up—it was just above my finger-tips—and suddenly my feet were knocked out from under me. I toppled backward over Bob's big, furry body.

I put out my hand to cushion the fall and crashed to the ground.

"Ow!" I rolled over on my side, holding my wrist. The pain was crushing.

"Lizard! Lizard!" Mary Ann got to me first. "Are you okay?"

"My wrist." The words came out in squeaks between gasps and cries I couldn't help.

Everyone crowded around me.

"Lizard!" Zach said, kneeling next to me. "Oh, Lizard." His face crumpled. If I hadn't been in so much pain, I would've given his arm a squeeze. I could see he felt terrible.

Mary Ann turned around to the others.

"Call her mom! We need to take her to the hospital!"

Even through that awful pain, I realized it: This was my ticket out of the fashion show. Who wants to see a model wearing a cast?

All right!

CHAPTER TWELVE

THE DOCTOR SAID MY wrist was fractured, and he put on a cast that went from my thumb to my elbow. Mary Ann, Sam, and Zach came to the emergency room with my mom and me.

While Mom talked with the doctor and Sam and Zach eavesdropped on the conversation, Mary Ann stood next to the table I sat on and looked sad.

"Mary Ann, cheer up," I said out of the corner of my mouth, so nobody else would hear. "Don't you know what this means?"

Mary Ann looked surprised and shook her head.

"Ms. Landers takes one look at this, and I'm out of the fashion show." I grinned.

Mary Ann's face lit up. "Hey, I didn't think of that."

"No modeling swimsuits. No hiccuping, nobody laughing at me or making fun."

"No Cubs game, either."

"I know, but even that isn't worth public humiliation."

"I guess not."

I took a deep breath and let it out. "I feel great. And I didn't even break my pitching wrist."

Zach came over. He looked terrible. "Lizard," he said in a soft voice. "I'm really sorry."

"It's not your fault, Zach," I said. "I should've looked where I was going. And I should've put Bob inside. He always wants to play in our games."

"I shouldn't have thrown it like that. I was mad."

"Because I yelled at you for that wild pass," I said. "I'm sorry I yell—"

"Oh, cut it out, Lizard," he said. "This is my fault."

"No, it's not. And it's not a big deal. Really."

"She's telling the truth, Zach," Mary Ann said.

I couldn't tell him that I was happy I'd

broken my wrist, but I didn't want him to feel guilty about it, either.

"Want to be the first to sign my cast?" I asked him. He grinned, and the nurse handed him a felt-tip pen.

He wrote: *I know I break you up, Lizard, but this is ridiculous.*

Everybody knew about my wrist by the time I got to school the next day. Ginger raced over as Mary Ann and I walked toward the building. Lisa and Heather followed close behind.

"Oh, Lizard!" Ginger cried. "It's terrible! I'm so sorry! It's bad to have to wear a cast, but the worst thing of all is that you'll probably be out of the fashion show!"

"I'll have to talk with Ms. Landers," I said.

Lisa smiled. "A model is supposed to be flawless."

"You said that about the scratches on Lizard's chin," Mary Ann said pointedly, "but she was picked to model, anyway."

"But nobody models with a cast," Ginger said. She put a hand sympathetically on my arm. "I'm sorry, Lizard."

Lisa looked very pleased about the whole

thing. "I wonder if I'll get to model the swim-suit?" she said. "I'd have to get a different size, of course."

She would have to point that out.

"Does it hurt?" Ginger asked.

"A little."

"You fell over your dog?" Lisa asked, her lips curling up in a wicked smile. "That's pretty funny."

I smiled sweetly. "You should try it some-time."

The bell rang and we headed into the school building.

I went to the rehearsal that night feeling pretty good. My last rehearsal, I thought. I told Mom to wait five minutes after dropping me off in case Ms. Landers said there was no reason for me to stay.

"I'll probably be right back," I said to Mom.

"I'm going to run into the bookstore, and that'll take a few minutes. If you're not back by then, I'll go on home."

"I'll be there," I said.

I hurried down to the empty store and walked over to Ms. Landers. Some of the girls pointed. "Look at Lizard!"

"One less to compete for Supermodel," someone whispered, and they giggled.

"Hi," I said to Ms. Landers.

She looked up from her ever-present notebook. "Hi, Liz—" She stopped, gawking at my arm. "What happened?"

"I broke my wrist playing football."

I saw Lisa edging over to us, eavesdropping.

Ms. Landers frowned. "Oh, my gosh. Are you okay?"

"I'm fine."

She scratched her head and seemed to be thinking hard.

"You probably don't want me to model in the show, right?"

"I'll model the swimsuit," Lisa blurted.

Ms. Landers turned to Lisa. "No, Lizard will model the swimsuit," she said firmly. She looked back at me. "Of course you're still in the show, Lizard. We'll have to make a few adjustments so you can get the garments on easily over your cast. You can't wear narrow sleeves, for instance. I'll have Samantha help you with your changes if you need it."

I couldn't believe it! "But a model's supposed to be flawless," I said.

"Who said that?" Ms. Landers asked, surprised.

"Lisa."

"That's baloney. A model should be attractive and graceful, but also human, with personality." She stared at me a moment. "Maybe we can even use this to our advantage."

Lisa *hmmmph*ed and stomped off.

It was fun seeing Lisa mad, but the panic was back, clutching at my throat. I was going to have to model the swimsuit. I couldn't believe it. I had a broken wrist, and it wasn't going to do me any good! It seemed that I was never going to figure out how to get out of the fashion show.

We went through the rehearsal as usual, practicing to the four songs. "Remember, ladies," Ms. Landers said at the end of the rehearsal, "the show is one week from tomorrow."

The other girls squealed with excitement. My stomach lurched.

"Lizard, tomorrow morning I'll choose outfits that'll work with your cast. Please go for your fittings between noon tomorrow and Sunday afternoon.

"Everyone, rehearsal will be here, as usual,

Monday evening. Think through the songs over the weekend so you won't be rusty on Monday. And don't anyone else break any bones before the show!"

Everyone laughed and looked at me. "I promise not to play football over the weekend!" Karen called out, laughing.

Right. Like she'd ever played a game of football in her whole entire life.

I went home, thinking how weird things can be. After I'd broken my wrist, I thought I'd be out of the fashion show. But here I was, still in the show, and Ms. Landers thought we could "use it to our advantage."

One step forward, two steps back.

CHAPTER THIRTEEN

SATURDAY MORNING MY stomach was filled with butterflies. I kept imagining myself modeling my swimsuit to that third song, with everybody laughing at me.

In the afternoon, I had to go to the mall for my fittings. Mom didn't want me riding my bike with my cast on my arm, so I had to convince her that I was perfectly capable of controlling my bike using my good right arm and the fingers on my left hand. I rode up and down the street in front of our house while she watched.

"See?" I said, shrugging as I passed her. "No problem."

"Okay," she said reluctantly. "But wear your helmet. And be careful!"

Mothers are funny about that. They always say "Be careful," as if their kids wouldn't be careful unless they said it.

I got to the mall with no problem. I was glad Ms. Landers had chosen the clothes with my cast in mind. The sleeves all went over it without a problem.

First were the jeans, polo, socks, and cross-training shoes at The Trap. They were really comfortable and fit fine. The manager was busy, but she said, "That looks great," when I stepped out of the dressing room to show her. If only I'd been assigned to wear those clothes through the whole show!

Then I went to Pearson's and tried on the denim skirt, blouse, and pumps. They weren't bad, and I figured I could handle wearing them in front of everybody if I didn't get the hiccups.

The next store was Claussen's, where I tried on the dressiest thing I'd ever worn, a red column dress. I thought I'd hate it because it was long and narrow, and I figured it would be uncomfortable. But when I put it on and looked in the mirror, I couldn't believe it was me! I looked about sixteen. It didn't matter that I was thin, because there were gathers in front that made me look . . . well, pretty good. In fact, the dress looked really good *because* I was thin.

"That's stunning!" the manager said when she saw me wearing it. "It looks wonderful on you." She smiled wryly, adding, "It would look even better without the cast."

I was beginning to feel a tiny bit better. I'd put off the swimsuit for last. But I had to try it on eventually, so with shaky knees, I walked to the end of the mall and into McCloud's Sporting Goods.

"I'm Lizard Flanagan," I said to the first woman I saw. "I need to try on the swimsuit for the fashion show."

"I don't work here, honey," she said, and she pointed to the person behind the counter. "Ask him."

A man!

Good grief, was he the manager? I looked at his name badge. JEFF WASHBURN, MANAGER, it said. I felt dizzy.

How could I show him how I looked in the suit?

He saw me staring at his badge. "Can I help you?"

"Uh . . . well, I'm here to try on a suit. You know, for swimming. A swimsuit. For the fashion show."

"Oh. Okay." He walked back to a rack of brightly colored swimsuits. "The woman from the fashion show came in this morning."

"Ms. Landers," I said.

"Right, Ms. Landers," he said. "She looked around and said you should pick one from this rack of competition suits."

"Do you . . . uh, do I need to show you?" He looked at me with a blank face. "Do you want to see what it looks like? *On,* I mean?"

"Oh, I don't think so. Just make sure it fits."

I blew out a breath I'd been holding. "Sure." What a relief.

"And bring it back to me so I can give it to Ms. Landers when she stops back here next week."

He went to the front of the store, and I looked through the rack of suits. I stopped at a pretty one, blue with red and white racing stripes. It was my size, so I took it to the dressing room and tried it on.

It fit and looked just the way I thought it would. Flat, flat, flat. I liked the racing stripes, though. Maybe some of the people in the audience would notice the stripes and not me.

I knew I wouldn't find a suit that looked any better, so I took it off, got dressed, and took it to the manager.

"I'll wear this one."

"Okay." He took it and tossed it onto a chair behind him.

That was that.

I walked out to my bike, climbed on, and headed toward home.

Three blocks from my house, I spotted Zach. He was walking along the sidewalk, holding a big cardboard box. He looked very serious as he crossed the grass toward the ravine.

I was curious about the box. And I was even more curious about the way Zach had been acting lately. I decided to follow him.

He ran down the side of the ravine and sat on the log at the bottom near the creek. I stopped at the edge behind a tree and watched.

Zach sat on the log for several minutes. Even from where I stood, I could see he was breathing hard. Then he did something sur-prising. He put the box over his head. Just for a second. Then he took it off.

He sat awhile longer, leaning his elbows

on his knees. Then he sat up straight and put the box over his head again. This time, he kept it on a second or two longer. Then he took it off again.

I thought about the last time Zach and I were in the ravine. He told me the story he'd made up about his uncle who was kept prisoner under the witch's porch.

That made me think about the story he'd told me about his baby-sitter locking him in the closet.

And that's when I understood why he'd been acting so funny lately. And why he was putting the box over his head.

I walked down the side of the ravine. He heard me tromping through the weeds and turned.

"Hi."

"Hi." Zach looked nervous, his eyes darting around and not looking at me. He was also sweating, even though it wasn't very hot.

I sat down on the fallen log with him.

"I just got back from trying on clothes for the fashion show."

"Oh." He fingered the box nervously.

"I'm still going to be in the show, even though I'm wearing the cast."

"That's good."

"No, it's not. I'm scared to death."

Zach looked at me. "You are? How come?"

"I'm scared of being in front of a crowd," I said. "I get stage fright, big time."

Zach frowned. "I didn't know that."

"In fourth grade I had to give a report, and I was so nervous, I started hiccuping and couldn't stop. I'm afraid that'll happen in the fashion show."

"Wow. I didn't know you were afraid of anything, Lizard," Zach said. "You always seem so, well, so brave and ready to try anything."

I smiled at him. "You wouldn't believe how scared I've been all week, just *thinking* about standing up in front of all those people!"

Zach seemed to relax a little. I think he was glad I told him about my fear. Then he frowned. "So what are you going to do?"

"I don't know. I guess I'm going to go through with it and hope I don't hiccup. And hope people won't laugh at me."

"Why would they laugh?" Zach asked.

I looked at the stream. "Maybe they'll think I'm really . . . thin, or something. I have to wear a—a swimsuit."

"I don't know why they'd laugh at that,"

Zach said. "You look great in a swimsuit."

"Really? Thanks, Zach." A good feeling about him was flooding into me. "You're a good friend."

Zach leaned his elbows on his knees, stared at the box, and sighed deeply.

"I've been scared lately too."

"What about?" I asked. I already knew, but I wanted him to tell me.

"Oh, you know how I'm playing *Dracula* in the scene at school?"

"Yeah."

"Well," he said, running his finger along the edge of the box, "I have to lie in a coffin for five minutes before I hear my cue."

"I bet it's kind of scary. Like your uncle getting locked up under the porch."

Zach turned to me. "That's it. That's it exactly. I hate being in small places. I'm claustrophobic, big time." His ears started turning pink. "I came here to sort of practice."

"That makes sense." I smiled. "I thought you were falling in love with Cassandra."

"Really?"

"I mean, her having such a nice neck and all. I think she's nice, too, but it made me sad. The kids have been saying that you want to be her boyfriend."

Zach frowned. "They have?"

I laughed. "You haven't been tuned in lately. That's what *everybody's* saying."

Zach shook his head. "Gee. All I've been thinking about is how horrible it'll be to lie in that box."

I grinned again. "You can't believe what a relief it is that you're not in love with her. But I'm sorry you're scared about the coffin. It's horrible being scared."

"Alan's dad is making the coffin for us," Zach said. "I climb out of it when Cassandra says, 'What a lovely night. The sky is filled with stars.' Boy, will I be waiting to hear those words!"

I sighed. "I'm glad I told you that I'm scared."

Zach grinned. "I'm glad I told you *I'm* scared. You're the only person who knows."

"Sort of makes it easier when you can talk about it, hunh?"

"Yeah," Zach said. "I'll be there in the front row at the fashion show, Lizard. When you get scared, look at me and I'll send you some 'calm down' vibes. And remember, I've seen you in a swimsuit hundreds of times."

"Thanks, Zach. And I'll be in the audience when you do your scene the next week. You won't be able to see me from inside the coffin, but I'll be sending you some 'calm down' vibes too."

Zach grinned. "Thanks, I'll need them."

I stood up and held out my hand. "Ready to go?"

"Yeah." He stood up too, and took my hand. "Let's go. I can practice with my box at home."

CHAPTER FOURTEEN

ALL THE NEXT WEEK, while we re-hearsed, I imagined myself wearing that swimsuit. I wondered if I'd be able to hear the music over all the laughing in the audience.

Then I thought about Zach sitting in the front row, sending me calming vibes. That made me feel good until I realized that Stinky would probably be sitting next to him, laughing his stupid head off.

Then I thought about Mom, Dad, Sam, Mary Ann, and Grandma sitting somewhere in the audience, the only serious—and red—faces in a sea of hysteria.

How would I ever get through it?

I also thought a lot about Zach. It would be horrible for him, lying in that closed, dark coffin, waiting for his cue to come out.

The girls in the fashion show started talking more and more about who would win the Supermodel contest. They were all going to the hair salon and getting their nails done.

Lisa showed up at school on Wednesday wearing ankle and wrist weights.

"Wow, Lisa," Ginger said, impressed. She'd arrived at our locker with Tiffany at her side. "Are you going to wear those during school?"

"Yes," Lisa said. "My mom's trainer says they're good for toning up. Of course, I'm not flabby, but I want to look my best."

Ginger nodded. "Especially when the fashion show is a mere three days away!"

It was funny that Lisa thought she could firm up her muscles in three days. Fortunately, though, I had my head in the locker, and they didn't hear me snicker.

Ginger grabbed her camera off the shelf and snapped a picture of me pulling books out of the locker.

I made a face. "Don't do that, Ginger."

"I've decided," she announced, "to document the days leading up to the fashion show. I'll make copies and put them in albums for us."

"I don't want any pictures," I said.

"But what if you're picked to be the Supermodel?" Ginger said. "This'll be your first modeling experience, the beginning of your career."

"What do you mean, what if Lizard is picked as Supermodel?" Lisa cried. "Some friend you are!"

"Well . . ." Ginger shrank back a little. "You never know."

"There's not going to be any career," I said. "Not for me."

"Especially wearing that cast," Lisa said. She turned to Tiffany, smirked, and said quietly, but loud enough for me to hear, "And that swimsuit."

She and Tiffany snorted and peeked at me to see if I was mad, while Ginger snapped a picture of them. I didn't give them the satisfaction of looking as if they were bothering me. I just pretended I didn't even hear, and walked away.

The only chance I had to talk with Zach alone was Thursday after school. We were waiting at the bike rack for Ed, Stinky, and Mary Ann. Sam had football practice.

"How are you doin'?" he asked me, squinting in the sun.

I was glad he asked. "Pretty nervous. Haven't you heard my knees knocking together?"

He grinned. "Nope. You'll be great. Ed and Stinky and I will cheer for you Saturday."

"Thanks. How are *you* doing?"

"I kept hoping the coffin wouldn't be finished by next Tuesday. But Alan said today that it's almost ready."

"Oh, sorry."

Ed and Stinky arrived then, so we stopped talking. We smiled at each other. It felt good to share a secret with Zach. I was glad he felt he could tell me about his claustrophobia. And I was happy that he'd be in the front row, cheering me on.

Now if I could just make it through the fashion show without hiccuping or throwing up because I was so nervous!

CHAPTER FIFTEEN

IT FINALLY CAME, THE DAY I'd been dreading. I woke up Saturday to see the sun slanting through my window and stretching across the floor of my room.

My heart started to race.

I got up, and as I made my bed, I thought, *The next time I lie in this bed, it'll all be over.*

I got dressed and thought, *Tomorrow morning when I get dressed, I won't be worried anymore.*

I made my breakfast and thought, *The next time I pour milk on my cereal, it'll all be behind me. Of course, I might never want to show my face in this town again.*

I ate only three bites of cereal. It felt as if the butterflies in my stomach were playing racquetball with the Cheerios, and I couldn't eat any more.

The fashion show was at two o'clock. We were supposed to be at the mall at noon.

I went upstairs and sat on my bed. I thought through the whole show, all the entrances, all the choreography. The show wasn't hard; I wasn't worried about that. It was all those eyes that would be out there watching.

Mom stuck her head in the door and smiled. "Hi, hon. Your big day is here! Grandma should arrive in a few minutes."

"Okay."

She left. I got up and went to my dresser. I picked up my comb and pulled it through my hair.

Hic.

I slapped a hand over my mouth. Oh, no! Please, not the hiccups!

I was breathing hard, waiting to see if there would be another one. Calm down, I said to myself. Just calm down.

Hic.

This was it, my worst nightmare. It was fourth grade all over again!

I ran down the hall and got a drink in the bathroom. I held my breath. *Hic.*

NO! I'd been through enough! The interview, the rehearsals, Ms. Landers saying I needed a bra, being humiliated when the clerk announced my size to practically the whole store. I'd even gotten into a fight with Lisa at rehearsal.

I shouldn't have to put up with anything else!

Hic.

I raced downstairs. "Mom, I've got the hiccups!"

Mom smiled. "Don't worry," she said. "They'll be gone by this afternoon."

"Don't bet the house on it."

She pulled a paper bag out from under the sink. "Put this over your head."

I did.

"Don't forget to breathe," Mom instructed.

"How could I forget to breathe?" I asked, my voice sounding loud in the sack.

The doorbell rang.

"There's Grandma," Mom said.

Hic.

"Mom, it's not working!" My voice boomed in my ears.

"I'm going to let her in," she said.

I stumbled through the dining room and into the foyer behind Mom. I heard the front door open.

"Hi, Mom," Mom said.

"Hello, dear," Grandma said. There was a pause. "Why does Lizard have a bag over her head?"

"Hi, Grandma," I said, and waved in what I figured was her general direction.

"Lizard has the hiccups," Mom said.

"Oh, we'll take care of those in a hurry," Grandma said.

"Great!" *Hic.*

"Take that bag off your head, Lizard, and come with me."

I pulled off the bag and followed her into the kitchen. Grandmas are supposed to know old-fashioned remedies for stuff, and my hopes were high that she'd help me get rid of these hiccups.

She took a glass from the cupboard and filled it with water. "Now, lean way over and drink the water upside down from the lower rim of the cup."

I leaned over and sipped the water. It dribbled out the corners of my mouth, across my cheeks, and into my ears.

Hic. The hiccup pulled some water into my windpipe, and I started coughing.

"You're not supposed to inhale the water, dear," Grandma said, slapping me on the back.

So much for old-fashioned remedies.

The telephone on the wall rang, and Mom picked it up. "It's for you, Lizard," Mom said.

I went to the phone. "Hello?"

"Lizard, this is Ginger. In the theater, you don't say 'Good luck,' you say, 'Break a leg.' So I hope you break all of your legs and all of your arms!" She laughed loudly.

"I only have two of each," I said. *Hic.*

"What was that?"

"What was what?" I didn't want to talk about my hiccups with Ginger. I just wanted to get off the phone and try and get rid of them.

Hic.

"That! You have the hiccups?" Ginger's voice rose. "You've *got* to get rid of them! What if you hiccup in the fashion show?"

"I've got to go, Ginger." *Hic.* I hung up.

"This is terrible, this is horrible, this is ridiculous!" I stomped into the living room.

"What's terrible, horrible, and ridiculous?" Sam asked. He sat in the living room, eating a banana. "I mean, besides you?"

"I have the hiccups! I can't stop them."

But if I thought my dear brother would try and help me, I was wrong. He just shrugged and loped out of the room.

I ran upstairs to the phone in my parents' room, so I could talk privately with Mary Ann. I dialed her number.

"Mary Ann," I said frantically. "It's happened." *Hic.* "I've got them."

"Oh, my gosh," she said. "Okay, listen. I prepared for this. In the last few days I've asked almost everybody I know how they get rid of hiccups. I've got my list right here. First, try taking a drink of water."

"I already tried that."

"Okay, next try holding your breath."

"I tried that too."

"Put a paper bag over your—"

"Didn't work."

"Did you take a tablespoon of sugar?"

"No. That's it? Just eat a tablespoon of sugar?"

"That's what my grandma said."

I was willing to take a chance on another

grandma. "Wait a second."

I dropped the phone and ran downstairs. Mom and Grandma were sitting in the living room.

"How are the hiccups?" Mom called.

Hic. "Alive and well."

I hurried into the kitchen and scooped out a tablespoon of sugar from the bowl on the table.

"BOO!"

My nerves were already pretty well shot, but when Sam leaped out at me from the dining room, I yelped and jumped a foot in the air, spilling the sugar all over the floor.

"Look what you made me do!" I yelled at him.

"Yeah, but are your hiccups gone?" he asked.

I waited. Five seconds passed. Then ten.

"They're gone! Sam, they're—" *Hic.* "They're still here."

I scooped out another spoonful of sugar and jammed it in my mouth for good measure. It was sweet and gritty and took a while to get down.

Hic.

I groaned and ran out of the kitchen.

"Clean up that sugar, will you, Sam?" I yelled over my shoulder, crunching sugar under my sneakers.

As I ran up the stairs, I heard him protesting that he was *not* going to clean it up because he wasn't the person who spilled it in the first place.

"It didn't work!" I wailed to Mary Ann.

"Okay, I have some more remedies," she said. "One of them has to work! Go stand on your head, and hold your breath as long as you can."

"Okay." I dropped the phone again and stood on my head next to my parents' bed. I took a big breath and held it a long, long time. My head felt full, as if all the organs in my body had slid down into my skull. I was sure my heart, lungs, stomach, and intestines were stuffed into my head like giblets in a Thanksgiving turkey. I saw a pair of feet walk into the room and heard someone's voice.

The next thing I knew, I was lying on the floor. Mom was kneeling over me.

"Lizard? Are you okay? You must've passed out."

"I don't feel too well." *Hic.* "Will you tell

Mary Ann I'll call her later? She's on the phone."

Mom talked to Mary Ann and hung up. "Why don't you lie down?" she suggested.

I got up slowly, walked into my room, and flopped on the bed.

"This is the worst day"—*hic*—"of my entire life," I said.

Mom and Grandma dropped me off at the mall. "I'm sure your hiccups will be gone by the time the show starts," Mom said.

"Hold your breath as much as you can," Grandma said.

"Don't tell her that!" Mom said. "She passed out this morning because she held her breath too long."

"Don't hold your breath, dear," Grandma said. "Your hiccups will probably stop by themselves."

Hic. "Sure, Grandma."

I said good-bye and ran in the mall entrance. Shoppers were milling around with their bags of stuff they'd bought. Some sat at tables at the food court near the entrance.

The stage and runway were set up in the

middle of the court. The backdrops were black so the clothes would show up well in front of them, I guessed.

I imagined myself up on that stage two hours from now, walking through that third song, wearing nothing but my swimsuit and sneakers.

Hic.

The hiccup echoed through the mall corridors, over the noise of the shoppers. People turned to look at me. Some smiled. I slapped a hand over my mouth and hurried toward Pearson's, where our dressing room was set up. I'd only been at the mall a few seconds, and already I was making a spectacle of myself.

Most of the other girls were already there. Some were fixing their hair, some their makeup. Ms. Landers was busy, moving around the room with her clipboard under her arm.

Lisa hurried over to me. "Ginger called," she said. "Did you get rid of your hiccups?"

Hic.

It was the loudest one yet. All the models stopped and turned to look at me.

I winced. "Hi," I said to everyone.

"Was that a hiccup?" Ms. Landers asked, hurrying toward me.

"Yes."

Lisa smirked.

"There's a drinking fountain at the end of the corridor—"

"I've drunk so much water, my back teeth are floating," I told her. I knew everyone was listening.

"When did you get them?"

"Two hours ago. Ms. Landers, I've tried everything. I put a bag over my head, ate sugar, held my breath, been scared silly, stood on my head, and drank water upside down."

Ms. Landers looked nervous. I guess she'd never had to deal with a hiccuping model before.

"Why don't you go get ready," she said. "Maybe they'll go away if you're thinking about something else."

Like modeling the swimsuit? I wondered. *Hic.*

Some of the girls snickered, and most of them looked pleased about the whole thing. Especially Lisa.

"Your makeup table is next to the wall over there, Lizard," Ms. Landers said.

I nodded and went to my table. I flicked on the switch, and the lights around the mirror flashed on.

I sat down and brushed out my hair.

Hic.

I arranged it in a French braid.

Hic.

I checked the order of my wardrobe changes on the aluminum rack next to my table.

Hic.

I filled the dressing area with my hiccups. They were getting worse. Closer together and louder than ever.

I felt tears in my eyes, but I forced a smile every time someone looked at me.

Ms. Landers hovered nearby and paced back and forth. I felt sorry for her. This was terrible for her too.

When my hair and makeup were done, I went to the entrance of Pearson's and looked out. I closed my lips tightly and put a hand over my mouth so if I hiccuped, I wouldn't make too much noise.

The mall was quickly filling up with people.

Mom, Dad, Sam, and Grandma sat in the fifth row. Mom and Grandma were talking, looking worried. Dad and Sam sat quietly, looking bored.

Ginger, Tiffany, and Heather sat in the second row, yakking away and laughing.

Zach had said he'd sit in the front row, but I didn't see him. I didn't see Ed or Stinky, either. Maybe they forgot. I didn't care. In fact, I hoped Zach wouldn't come. I didn't want him to see my public humiliation.

I went back to my table and sat down. *Hic.* We weren't supposed to sit in the clothes we were modeling, so no one was dressed yet.

Hic.

Abby came over. "I'm sorry about your hiccups, Lizard," she said. "I'm sure you'll do fine. The hiccups probably won't be heard past the fifth or sixth row, anyway. I mean, with the music playing and all."

She was trying to be nice, so I smiled. "Thanks. I hope you're right."

"We have twenty minutes left," Ms. Landers called out. "Please put on your first outfit. And don't forget to use your pillowcases."

Hic.

Ms. Landers shot me a worried look.

We'd each had to bring a pillowcase from home. It was to protect the clothes from getting makeup on them. Ms. Landers had said if we got any makeup on the clothes, the store wouldn't take them back, and we'd have to buy them.

I put my pillowcase over my head, then pulled on the polo.

I changed into the jeans, socks, and cross-training shoes, hiccuping the whole time. Then I walked to the entrance and looked out again.

The audience was twice as large now.

"Lizard!" It was a whisper to my right.

"Oh, Zach." He stood there, smiling. It was so good to see his face!

Hic.

"I heard about your hiccups."

"It's horrible. I don't know what to do." *Hic.* "This is the worst thing that's ever happen—"

Before I knew what was happening, Zach pulled me to him and kissed me full on the mouth. It was warm and tingling, and I felt myself go limp.

We came up for air, and then he kissed me again. Long and sweet.

When he finally pulled away, I realized I was breathless. I blinked at him.

"Feel better?" he asked.

"I— well, I— It's just that— I mean, we've never—" I couldn't get the words out.

"They're gone, aren't they?"

"What's gone?"

"The hiccups. They're gone."

I waited about ten seconds. Fifteen. I took a big breath and let it out. No hiccups.

"Wow. They *are* gone." I looked at him. "Thanks!"

Zach grinned, his ears bright red. "See you after the show. Good luck." He squeezed my hand and disappeared.

I looked up to see Lisa standing there. She looked furious. She must have seen the whole thing.

I laughed. "Come on, Lisa," I said. "We've got a show to do!"

CHAPTER SIXTEEN

I **COULDN'T BELIEVE HOW** fast the show went. The first two songs zipped by. I didn't even have to think about the choreography because we'd been through it so many times.

Besides, all I could think about was Zach and his amazing hiccup remedy. I could tell he was really feeling that kiss, like I was. It was a sensational kiss. The kiss of a lifetime. A major hiccup-stopping kiss. I was looking forward to getting another one, even if I didn't have the hiccups.

Zach sat in the front row, just as he'd promised. He grinned at me, and I grinned back during the first two songs. Then I smiled at Mary Ann and Mom and Dad and Grandma and Sam and Ed.

I even smiled at Stinky—for just a second.

I was still feeling great when I put on the swimsuit. *Just do it,* I thought. *Don't even think about it.*

When I heard my cue, I bounced out on-stage to the music, holding my head up, swinging my arms a little and grinning. A huge whoop went up from the crowd. I laughed and waved to them with the arm in the cast. They whooped even louder.

All that worry for nothing! I grinned all the way through that song, and before I knew it, it was over.

In the last song, when I came out in that sophisticated column dress, Zach looked impressed. Ginger put two fingers in her mouth and whistled. Everyone seemed to be looking at me and smiling because my cast didn't quite fit the elegance of the dress.

And that was it. The fashion show was over, and, believe it or not, I was just a tiny bit sorry to have it end. I had dreaded it so much, and it had turned out to be fun! My hiccups didn't come back, and no one had laughed.

Ms. Landers asked the audience to re-main seated while the judges' ballots were tallied to determine the winner of the Supermodel prize. Then she called all of us to come back onstage. We were still dressed in our evening wear. We stood together and waited. I grinned again at Zach, and even from the stage, under the bright lights, I could see his ears turn red. It made me smile even more.

Mom and Dad and Grandma looked happy. Mom gave me a thumbs-up sign, and Mary Ann gave me an A-okay sign.

"Ladies and gentlemen," said Ms. Landers into the mike at stage right, "the judges have made their decision. The Supermodel is chosen not only for her beauty and ability to model fashions, but also for the mood she creates with the music and the personality that she projects from the stage.

"This year, the judges have selected as the Spring Pines Fashion Show Supermodel"— the mall was absolutely quiet, waiting—"a young lady who deserves this title: Lizard Flanagan."

For a second the whole world stopped. Then a roar went up from the crowd, and hands pushed me forward, and I looked out over the mob of people who clapped and stood up and clapped some more. Zach beamed and whooped, and Mary Ann's eyes sparkled, and it seemed that the whole world was watching me.

Could this really be happening? Maybe it was a mistake . . .

I don't remember getting there, but suddenly I was standing next to Ms. Landers. She handed me a certificate and a check and shook my hand, then gave me a big hug. I grinned and waved to the crowd, who smiled and waved back.

And it was over.

It was *over*!

But *wow*! What an ending!

"Well, I can tell you one thing. Lisa wasn't even in the running for Supermodel," Mary Ann said that evening. "She scowled through the whole show."

Mary Ann and I were sitting under the maple tree in the backyard.

I grinned. I'd been grinning most of the time since the show. I'd grinned while everybody congratulated me on my Supermodel award; I'd grinned while I took off my makeup and changed back into my regular clothes; I'd grinned while I ate my celebration dinner out with my family and while I said good-bye to Grandma.

And now I grinned again. "You want to know why Lisa was so crabby during the show?"

"Sure. Why?"

I peered up into the tree to make sure Sam wasn't up there, listening.

"Want to know how I really got rid of my hiccups?" I'd told everyone after the show that they'd stopped by themselves.

"How?"

I leaned closer to Mary Ann. "Zach kissed me."

Mary Ann's eyes got big, and her mouth opened in a huge O. "Really? What was it like?"

So I told her all about it. How I was in such a panic about the hiccups, how he appeared like magic outside the dressing area. And how he pulled me to him and kissed me. Twice.

"Twice?"

"Twice." I grinned some more. "He has nice lips." That last comment just slipped out, and I slapped a hand over my mouth, laughing.

"And your hiccups stopped?"

"Instantly."

"Just think," Mary Ann said. "You'll remember your first kiss for the rest of your life. The kiss that saved the fashion show."

"Yeah, really."

"And earned you the Supermodel prize." Mary Ann sat back against the tree. "I wondered why you were so sparkly up there on the stage."

"I was sparkly?"

"Awesomely sparkly."

"I'm never doing it again."

"You don't have to. And now we can sign up for the Wrigley Field trip."

"Yeah, it'll be so awesome. Plus, I can pay my parents back and still have fifty dollars left over."

But then I remembered that before we went to Chicago, Zach had to go through something that was as scary to him as the fashion show was for me.

He had to lie in that closed, dark coffin in his *Dracula* scene. I wished there was something I could do to help him the way he helped me. Somehow I knew that it was going to take more than a kiss to solve *his* problem.

* * *

The idea came to me after school on Monday, the day before Zach had to do his scene. I'd run out of sport socks, so I went into my parents' room to borrow a pair from my mom. On the bedside table was my dad's little cassette player and earphones and two tapes he'd been listening to.

"That's it!" I said, and scooped them up.

When I explained it to Mom, she said I could borrow them for a day. Then I ran over to Zach's house and told him what to do.

He looked doubtful but said, "I'll try anything."

I was almost as nervous for Zach as he was. After school Tuesday, practically the whole sixth grade showed up in the Little Theater to see the scenes.

There were three scenes to be presented. *Dracula* was last.

I felt a lot of eyes on me when Mary Ann and I sat down in the front row. Lisa obviously hadn't told anyone about Zach kissing me, and everyone still thought he was in love with Cassandra. They were all waiting to see him bite her neck.

Ginger and Heather came in and sat

down next to me. "Sure you want to sit in the front row?" Ginger asked me sympathetically.

I smiled at her. "Sure."

She looked surprised, and I winked at Mary Ann, who grinned back.

The first two scenes were pretty good, I guess, but I didn't pay a whole lot of attention to them. I kept thinking about Zach backstage, probably in a cold sweat, waiting to start his scene in the coffin. I sure hoped my idea worked.

Finally, it was time for the *Dracula* scene. The curtain opened. The stage was set up in two parts. The left side was the cellar, and the right side was an old-fashioned parlor.

On the floor of the cellar was a crate. Lying across the crate was the closed coffin. Zach must be inside it now, I thought. Oh, I hoped my idea would work!

Cassandra, wearing a long gown, stood in the parlor talking to Al Pickering, who played her father.

"Father, dear, you needn't be afraid to leave me alone tonight," she said. "I shall be quite all right. Nothing evil can befall me. The housekeeper is here, after all, and I'm going to spend the final hours of the day reading."

"Very well, my dear," Al said. He had a phony mustache pasted above his lip, and it bounced when he talked. Mary Ann pressed a hand over her mouth so she wouldn't laugh. "I shouldn't be too late." He walked stiffly to Cassandra and planted a kiss on her forehead. The kids in the audience laughed and a few of them hooted, "Oooooo!" He walked offstage.

Cassandra had some lines all by herself, imagining the man of her dreams. I kept looking at the coffin on the other side of the stage, thinking about Zach lying there inside. Was he okay?

Cassandra danced around the room with an invisible partner, telling him how she had dreamed of this night.

Finally, she moved downstage, right in front of me. She pantomimed opening the window. She looked out over the audience and said, "What a lovely night. The sky is filled with stars."

That was Zach's cue! Now he'd get to climb out of that dark, awful coffin. I watched the lid of the coffin, waiting for him to lift it and get out.

Nothing happened.

Cassandra waited, still gazing out over the audience. Her eyes darted sideways; she was probably trying to see if Zach was coming toward her.

The audience was silent.

Zach's teacher, Mrs. Brown, sat in the front row. "Say the line again," she whispered to Cassandra. "Maybe he didn't hear you."

Cassandra nodded and raised her voice. "What a lovely night. The sky is filled with stars."

Still nothing happened.

What was wrong with Zach? Had the fright of being in the coffin paralyzed him?

Cassandra shifted her weight over one foot and looked uncomfortable. She frowned, then said very loud, "I said, *What a lovely night! The sky is filled with stars!*"

Nothing. A murmur ran through the crowd.

I had a terrible thought. What if Zach couldn't breathe in there? What if the lid was so heavy—

"IT SURE IS A GREAT-LOOKING NIGHT OUT THERE!" hollered Cassandra. "LOOK AT ALL THOSE STARS, JUST HANGING RIGHT UP THERE IN THE SKY!"

The coffin lid was suddenly thrown back, and Zach, looking sleepy-eyed and sluggish, hauled himself out of the coffin.

I couldn't believe it. Zach had fallen asleep!

The audience was nearly in a frenzy, knowing what was going to happen next. Zach pantomimed creeping up the stairs, then he tiptoed into the parlor.

He crept up behind her and opened his mouth. Two long, pointy fangs hung down. He drew her neck toward him and Cassandra rolled her eyes impatiently as if she was thinking, *It's about time you got here!*

Zach pretended to bite deep into her neck, and the audience went crazy, whistling and clapping. I hooted louder than anyone! Ginger looked over at me, surprised.

Cassandra slumped into Zach's arms, and as the curtain went down, the audience was on its feet, hooting and applauding.

The curtain came back up. The cast took their bows, and Zach looked right at me and winked. I winked back and laughed.

Ginger looked over at me again.

I shrugged at her, grinned, and clapped till my hands turned red.

CHAPTER SEVENTEEN

THIS TIME ON SATURDAY, we'll be sitting in the stands at Wrigley Field," I said, swishing a long stick in the stream. Zach and I sat on the log at the bottom of the ravine.

"Stuffing our faces with hot dogs and popcorn," he said.

"And watching the best baseball players in the world. I'm going to get Mark Grace's autograph."

"Maybe we'll catch a fly ball," Zach said. "Would that be cool, or what?"

I sighed and watched the water sparkle in the late afternoon sun.

"I can't believe the fashion show is over," I said.

"You were great," Zach said. "And thanks for your dad's relaxation tape. I didn't think it would work, but I made myself concentrate on it."

"And you fell asleep!"

"Yeah." Zach grinned. "It worked great."

We didn't say anything for a moment.

"Zach?"

"Yeah?"

"You know how you stopped my hiccups?"

"Yeah."

"How did you know it would work?"

"I didn't," Zach said. "I just thought I'd try it." He grinned again, and this time his ears turned red. "You didn't mind, did you?"

"Gee, no," I said. I could feel a dopey grin taking over my face. "It was fun. I mean, it was nice."

"Yeah, it was." He stared into the water, smiling.

"Hey, Zach?"

"Hunh?"

"Wouldn't it be funny if it worked the other way?"

He turned and looked full into my face. "What do you mean?"

"I mean, if you *didn't* have the hiccups, and you . . . sort of kissed someone, and you *got* the hiccups? Like a toggle switch?"

207

Zach laughed. "Yeah, that'd be pretty funny."

I moved a little closer to him and said softly, "You want to try it?"

Zach blinked and caught his breath. "Sure."

I tipped my head a little to avoid bumping noses with him. He tipped his head in the same direction. Then we both tipped in the other direction.

"I'll go this way, you go that way," he said.

I nodded.

We both leaned in and kissed gently. I felt something like an electrical charge rush up and down my body, but I didn't hiccup.

When he gently pulled away, I said, "Let's try one more time."

We kissed again. Still no hiccups.

Then we both said at the same time, "So it's not like a toggle switch," and we laughed.

Zach reached up and touched my cheek. "I just realized something: I'm kissing a supermodel. That's really cool."

"My modeling days are over, Zach."

"That's okay." Zach grinned. "I wouldn't mind kissing you if you weren't a super-model. It's pretty fun."

I grinned back. "As much fun as playing football?"

"Yeah."

"I think so too," I said. "What about baseball?"

"Hmmm," he said. "I'll have to think about that."

I leaned over and kissed him one more time, just to help him make up his mind.

"Well," he said, "it's a *real* close second to baseball."

I laughed. "Real close."

"Maybe even tied for first," he said.

"Yeah, that's it," I agreed. "Tied for first."

CAROL GORMAN is the author of many books for young readers, including THE MIRACULOUS MAKEOVER OF LIZARD FLANAGAN, an ABA Pick of the Lists, CHELSEY AND THE GREEN-HAIRED KID, an ALA Recommended Book for Reluctant Young Adult Readers, and JENNIFER-THE-JERK IS MISSING.

Although she wasn't a tomboy when she was young, she loved climbing trees and never owned a doll.

Ms. Gorman lives in Iowa with her husband, who is also a full-time writer.